THE SEAL OF YUEH LAO

Novels by John Michael Greer

The Weird of Hali:

Ariel Moravec Occult Mysteries:

Others:

THE SEAL OF YUEH LAO

A Fantasy with Shifting Shapes

John Michael Greer

AEON

Published in 2024 by
Aeon Books

British Library Cataloguing in Publication Data

A C.I.P. for this book is available from the British Library

ISBN-13: 978-1-91595-204-2

Cover art by Margaux Carpio
Typeset by Medlar Publishing Solutions Pvt Ltd, India

www.aeonbooks.co.uk

CONTENTS

CONTENTS

CHAPTER 1

THE STONES OF ELK HILL

"Do it again," said the old woman. "Now."

Asenath Merrill stifled an irritable response, turned her attention back to the bowl of water on the old wooden table in front of her. Sixteen that summer, she had curling brown hair—tied back just then for convenience—and a body in that awkward place, no longer a girl's, not quite a woman's, that didn't quite suit the homespun blouse and skirt she wore and wouldn't have suited anything else better. Her violet eyes looked black in the dim light.

Around her, Betty Hale's kitchen seemed to lean inward, as though watching her in the yellow glow of the oil lamp. Bundles of herbs tied up with twine hung from hooks screwed into the ceiling beams; the wood stove to one side, a big cast iron model more than a century old, had a blackened pot simmering on a back burner, sending up curls of steam that smelled of strange roots and mushrooms. Betty herself, lean and wrinkled and white-haired, dressed in a cotton house dress with a cardigan over it, looked on with an inscrutable expression. The window next to the table stood open, letting in chill air and a flood of pale moonlight.

The gibbous moon's reflection hovered in the water, a thin slice of its lower part still blotted out by a blackness that marked one of the old gray hills east of the little village

1

of Chorazin. Asenath made herself relax into the chair, slowed her breathing, stilled her thoughts, and tried to reach the state of mind, close to the edge of sleep but not over it, that would allow images to coalesce out of voor, the life force at the heart of witchcraft.

She had almost managed the trick when a dark blotch appeared near the upper left edge of the moon's reflection. Startled, she blinked, and the blotch vanished. She fought her way back to the state she needed, watched the blotch stretch into a line, the line turn into the first stroke of a letter in a script that was far older than the human race.

"There's a message," she said.

Betty came over to stand behind her and looked down at the bowl. "Why, so there is." She turned, got a yellowing paper notepad, a couple of cheap ballpoint pens, and a disk of polished silver a few inches across. "Copy it down, if it's for anyone here."

That, at least, took skills Asenath had learned a long time before. She took the silver disk, set it in the moonlight, adjusted it and herself so that she could see the moon gleaming on its surface, and murmured three strange words over it. A familiar motion traced a different Aklo character on the silver disk. She turned her attention back to the bowl of water, settled back into the almost-trance as Betty moved away again.

A moment passed before other marks appeared on the moon's reflection, but appear they did: ordinary letters forming words in English. She copied the letters one at a time, let out a little cry when she'd gotten enough of them to guess the rest of the first sentence.

"What is it?" Betty asked.

"It's for me," said Asenath, beaming.

"Keep copying," Betty replied, imperturbable.

One of the pens interfered with that by running dry halfway through a letter—that happened often enough, now that ballpoint pens had gotten scarce and those that could be found were shoddily made–and Asenath simply set it aside and picked up the other. She kept copying until the message was finished, then traced a character over the silver disk to let the sender know it had arrived and been copied in full. Still beaming, she handed the paper to Betty, who glanced over it and handed it back.

"Almost here, eh?" the old woman said. "I should have guessed that from yesterday's omens. Well, you can tell Walt Moore tomorrow." She gave Asenath a sidelong look. "I'm going to guess this'll give you a bit of trouble concentrating."

"Probably," Asenath admitted.

"You'll have to learn better." Betty shook her head. "Still, you might as well get a little sleep now. There's moly to be gathered on the hill first thing before the dew dries, and you won't be much use if you're blinking and yawning all the while."

Asenath said something agreeable, and then spent the necessary quarter hour dissolving the spells on bowl and silver disk and getting both washed and put in their places: one of her chores, and also part of her training. By the time she'd finished that, gone outside to wash up in cold water from the backyard pump and use the little house on the far end of the backyard, and picked her way beneath stars to the back door and then through darkness to her cramped little room, she was blinking and yawning enough to make Betty's words seem like a prophecy.

A trickle of moonlight came in through the lace curtains screening the room's one window, but she didn't need light at all to sense the little furry shape, about the size of a large rat, curled up on the middle of the pillow at one end of the narrow bed. She gave it an amused look, then settled on a bare wooden chair, regarded the pale statue of a woman-breasted cat on the dresser, and said her prayers to her goddess. Finishing, she turned to the shape on the pillow. "Come on, Rachel," she told it. "You don't get to hog the whole pillow."

The shape let out a sleepy chirring sound, then uncurled itself and padded over to the far side of the bed while Asenath shed her clothes, pulled on her nightgown, and crawled beneath the covers. As soon as she was settled, the creature picked its way back over to her and nestled down in the hollow between her upper arm and her breast.

"No, you can't go back to sleep," Asenath said. "I need to go someplace, remember?"

That got her a more plaintive chirr, but after a moment the creature blinked fully awake, turned its attention to the image in Asenath's mind, let out a little chuff, and then settled into a curious throaty churr Asenath knew well. She closed her eyes and let the moon-edged blackness of the waking world dissolve around her.

* * *

Wind on the stark hills of Rokol roused her from something that wasn't sleep. She sat up slowly, to give Rachel time to clamber up onto her shoulder, then got her woolen cloak settled about her to keep off the dawn chill. A twisted pine bent over her, sheltering. Further down the slope the woods grew thick, and shreds of fog twined about the trees. Behind her the first pale light of dawn spread across the sky, where Ilek-Vad rose in the distance. High above, a vast golden moon stood at first quarter. Asenath looked up at it, wondered about the cats.

Rachel let out a reproving chirr, and Asenath glanced at her and said, "No, I won't go find out." Cats and kyrrmis, the odd little primate species to which Rachel belonged, didn't get along at all, in the waking world or in the Dreamlands: kyrrmis thought cats were insufferable snobs and feared their teeth and claws; cats thought kyrrmis were shameless sycophants toward humans and didn't like to get close to those deft primate hands, so good at yanking tails and whiskers or jabbing at sensitive places. Asenath was used to the mutual dislike, and only now and then regretted that she could never visit Ulthar or leap to the moon.

She got to her feet, found the trail she'd been following the night before. Most dreamers had to risk the passage down the seventy steps to the cavern of flame where the priests Nasht and Kaman-Tha make strange offerings to the gods of dream, and then down the seven hundred steps to the Gates of Deeper Slumber and the Enchanted Wood beyond, but she did not. The curious gifts the folk of drowned Poseidonis had bred into kyrrmis in ages long past gave Asenath the trick of entering the same dream night after night, finding herself each time where she'd left off before. During the long years when kyrrmis had been thought to be lost forever, the worshipers of the Great Old Ones had done without that power, but a few people had begun to reclaim it. Asenath was neither the first or the most daring of them—those titles belonged to a friend she planned to meet in Ooth-Nargai soon—but she'd become a skilled dreamer in the eight years since Rachel had come into her life, and made more than one discovery in the Dreamlands that had made a difference in the waking world.

The trail led a little south of west out of Rokol's crags into the lower and more thickly forested Hills of Hap. The maps she'd studied in Ilek-Vad showed the trail passing far enough north of the Eastern Desert's edge that she didn't have to worry about coming too close to the ruins of Bethmoora and the red-footed wamps that haunted them. As she headed down the trail she made a point of turning right whenever it forked, toward the nearby shores of the Twilight Sea and away from the desert. Even so, though the trail seemed to run straight, the morning sun veered oddly as she walked, shining more and more on her left side. Rachel let out a low worried chirr; she responded with a nod, slipped a hand into the leather satchel she wore, and readied a periapt that had certain powers against red-footed wamps.

Bur it wasn't a red-footed wamp that waited for her when, as she had begun to expect, the trail came within sight of the first tumbledown ruins of Bethmoora. Tawny and languid, a sphinx stretched its leonine body atop the moss-covered remnants of a wall, lifted its woman's head, gazed at her with half-lidded eyes. Asenath stopped and waited politely for the sphinx to speak.

It regarded her for a long moment, then said, "Who are you, that walk so boldly past the stones of fallen Bethmoora?"

The Seven Cryptical Books of Hsan warn earnestly of the dangers of telling one's name to a sphinx, and even at sixteen, Asenath was too knowledgeable a dreamer to be caught so easily. She answered instead in riddling words of the kind sphinxes cannot resist: "I am a child of earth and sea," she said, "and my grandmother is of the woods."

The sphinx lashed its tail. "Whence do you come?"

"From a city that's one and yet two and a friend who's a king and yet not a king."

The tail snapped back and forth again. "And whither do you go?"

"To a place where a woman who was old long before you were born will be a little child long after you're gone. I have friends there too."

The tail lashed again, but the sphinx bowed its head, conceding defeat. "What do you wish from me?"

"Wisdom," said Asenath, "and your blessing."

"You are bold," said the sphinx. After a pause: "But my blessing I give to you. As for the other—" It let out a low hissing breath. "I see the maker of moons, waiting for you. I see an old and bitter wrong that will not be righted while the world lasts. I see another, not so bitter and not so old, that you might help set right. I see—" Another long hissing breath filled the pause that followed. "I see a city of bridges and bells, and a child who waits there. Ah! She will return, and you will see her!"

All at once the sphinx sprang. Asenath, taken by surprise, was knocked down before she could react. Two great paws pressed her shoulders down, and the weight of the creature's body pinned her in place. The woman's face bent over hers, staring down with cat's eyes.

"You will see her," the sphinx said. "Watch for her. It will not be long."

Another bound, and the sphinx was back up on the wall, leaving Asenath shaken but unhurt. "It will not be long," the creature hissed at her and then bounded away.

Asenath sat up after a moment and extended an arm to Rachel, who had leapt to safety on the ground. The kyrrmi climbed up the proffered arm, chirred. "Yes, it was rude of her," Asenath agreed. "Sphinxes are like that." Rachel chirred again, and Asenath scrambled to her feet and tried to figure out the best way to avoid going through the rest of Bethmoora's ruins—the red-footed wamps were still much on her mind. Of course it turned out that all she had to do was try to veer toward the ruins, and she found herself moving inexorably away from them. The Hills of Hap rose around her, green with ginkgos and cypresses, and in due time the trail wound down out of the hills to a low bluff overlooking the Twilight Sea.

All the while, her thoughts circled around the words of the sphinx. The maker of moons, she thought. A city of bridges and bells. Though she'd spent years already studying classic texts of eldritch lore—the *Necronomicon*, of course, the *Book of Eibon*, and more recently *The Seven Cryptical Books of Hsan*—those titles roused no least hint of recollection. She shook her head, turned west to follow the coast toward Ogrothan and the Tanarian Hills.

* * *

Dawn found Asenath on top of Elk Hill, waiting for the sun to rise far enough over the hills east of Chorazin to touch the blossoms of a clump of red-flowered moly with its rays. The tips of the nine tall stones atop the hill were already incandescent with the sun's first red rays by the time she and Betty Hale got there, but scraps of mist still curled around Chorazin in its valley and Huntey Creek on the hill's far side. From below,

Asenath could hear the bleating of goats waiting impatiently to be fed and milked: a familiar sound to her, and even more so than usual just then, since she'd taken care of Betty's two nannies before they headed up the hill.

That wasn't the only sound there on the hilltop. Fitful breezes among the tall stones made a murmur like distant voices, sometimes rising into a shrill piping, sometimes falling away into a low hiss, but always present. The voice of the Alala, the old lore called it, and Asenath knew spells that could make it intelligible, though those had dangers of their own and were not to be used except at great need. She ignored the voices, watched the sun's crimson glow on the stones creep slowly down them, turning orange as it went, tried to learn patience. A glance at Betty, who had learned that lesson long before Asenath was born, didn't help matters any.

Finally the sunlight brushed the very tips of the moly blossoms. Another glance at Betty got a silent nod, and Asenath knelt by the plant and used the little crescent bronze knife she carried to snip one flowering stalk of every six, placing her harvest in the basket beside her. A rhyme of lore she'd learned from her first teacher circled through her mind:

> One out of six from the red-flowered moly,
> One out of nine from the white;
> Gather the first as the sun dries the dew,
> Gather the last when the moon, thin and new,
> Shines on the leaves in the night.

Finishing, she murmured the traditional prayer to the Black Goat of the Woods, thanking her for the gift of the plant, and stood up. There were two other clumps of red-flowered moly on the top of Elk Hill, but it grew nowhere else for many miles around and it was a courtesy to other witches to spare some for them. Eight stalks would have to do.

"Good," said Betty. "Now name me every other herb you see atop this hill and tell me what you can do with them."

It was a familiar drill, part of the discipline witches had practiced through the centuries when it was too dangerous to possess the old tomes or even their own notebooks of lore, and Asenath had learned to expect it. She rattled off all the herbs that she knew could be found there on the hilltop, each with its properties, then started looking for any that weren't so obvious, and found one, a silvery-gray, inconspicuous plant with narrow leaves and tiny white flowers. "And narrowleaf thieveswort, which will open a locked door if you repeat Eibon's spell for that, and makes you hard to see if you carry it on your right side," she finished, kneeling beside the inconspicuous herb. Then, trying to suppress a smile: "How did I do?"

Betty didn't answer. Asenath looked up, surprised. Her teacher had turned to face in toward the center of the stone circle, and after a moment Asenath looked the same direction.

There beside the tallest stone in the center was a girl a year or so younger than Asenath, thin and bony, wearing a plain dress of blue cotton that looked as though it had been slept in much more than once. Her feet were bare, and her hair, which was brown and straight, looked as if it hadn't been brushed in weeks. She glanced from side to side as though bewildered. Asenath rose from beside the herb, puzzled, for she knew all the daughters of the Chorazin folk and the girl wasn't one of them.

"Child," said Betty, "what are you doing up here?"

The girl started at the sound of the old woman's voice, gave her a terrified look, and then crumpled to the ground, covering her head with her hands. Betty went over to her and knelt, resting a hand on her shoulder; the girl jumped at the contact. "Don't you be afraid of me, child," Betty said then in a gentler voice. "Let's first of all get you outside the circle."

Though she was trembling visibly, the girl let Betty draw her to her feet and lead her out through a gap between two of the stones. She started again when she saw Asenath, but seemed to take some comfort in the presence of another girl.

Asenath came over and stood nearby. "Now, child," said Betty, sitting her down and then sitting on the moss in front of her. "Why don't you tell me your name?"

The girl swallowed visibly and said, "Cassie."

Betty paused, waiting, then asked, "And what's your family name?" That got her only a frightened look, and Betty went on: "Well, never mind that. How did you get up here on Elk Hill? You should know it's not a safe place to be."

"I don't know," Cassie said. "I—" She stopped in confusion, went on. "I went outside my stepfather's house."

"What's your stepfather's name?"

"I—I don't know. He's my stepfather, that's all."

"Where does he live?"

"In a little house in the woods. I live there too."

"And that's where you were when you went outside."

Cassie started trembling again. "Y—yes."

"And what happened between there and here?"

"I don't know." Her voice rose, unsteady. "I don't know. Where—where is here?"

"You're up on top of Elk Hill," said Betty. "The town of Chorazin's on one side of us and Huntey Creek's on the other."

The girl looked at her as though the names were in some alien tongue. "I don't know those names. I don't know this place. I want to go home." Tears trickled down her face.

Betty pulled a handkerchief from a pocket and handed it to Cassie, who gave her a baffled look but used it to mop her eyes. "Once we can figure out where your home is we'll get you there," said the old woman. "For now, why don't you come down the hill with me? Let's get you something to eat and drink, and then see if we can find your stepfather." She stood and turned to Asenath. "Sennie, you should let Walt know we've found a child from outside roaming up here on the hill. He'll know what to do. Go ahead and leave the moly; I'll bring it."

* * *

The brambles that hedged in the hilltop and covered the flanks of the hill in a green blanket weren't ordinary brambles, but then nothing on Elk Hill was quite ordinary. Asenath had grown up with stories about what the brambles had been like until a few months after she was born. Back in the days when terrible sorceries lay knotted in the depths of the hill and the ruins of the old van der Heyl house south of it, the flanks of the hill were covered with brown leafless brambles with savage thorns, which shifted and moved of themselves. Now the brambles were green and more than half hidden under great splayed leaves. In the spring the whole hill was one great murmur as bees danced from blossom to blossom, and after Asenath went home at summer's end there would be berries in such profusion that everyone in Chorazin would pick and process them for weeks, and trade jars of jam and bottles of berry wine thereafter to the people in less fortunate towns as far away as Maine. The brambles still moved of themselves, though, and so when Asenath found no gap in them, she faced them and said, "I'd like to go back down, please." Then: "And thank you for the moly. Miss Hale and I are both grateful."

A rustling sound a few paces further north told her that the brambles were pleased. Sure enough, a trail began there and curved down out of sight in a graceful leaf-lined arc. Asenath thanked the brambles and set off down the hill, half of her noting where the trail was leading her—it wasn't wise to wander Elk Hill without paying attention, the brambles might up and decide to take you far out of your way—and half puzzling over the girl who'd appeared so suddenly on the hilltop and who didn't know how she'd gotten there.

You didn't see many outsiders near Chorazin, not any more. People in Betty's generation talked about the days when when the county seat at Emeryville fifteen miles north was a thriving town, Pine Center ten miles closer wasn't just a clutch of abandoned houses falling in on themselves, and teenagers from both would drive through Chorazin now and then to shout insults and throw rocks from their car windows. The economic crisis had hit western New York hard, and there weren't many people left, not outside of the scattered villages where people worshiped the old gods of Nature. Were Cassie and her stepfather among the exceptions, living in an isolated farmhouse long after all their neighbors had gone looking for jobs out west? That seemed reasonable at first glance, less so when she thought about it, for how could Cassie have come from so far away she'd never heard Chorazin's name and not known how she got there?

The trail let Asenath out onto the old parking lot beside the Elk Hill Motor Hotel. The asphalt paving was cracked and potholed, well on its way back to oil-stained gravel, but it hadn't been in much better condition at the time of her first memories of Chorazin a decade back. She cut across the lot to the back door that led into the manager's apartment, went right in, plopped down on one of the chairs by the kitchen table, and called out, "Mr. Moore? I've got a message for you—well, actually, two of them."

"Just a moment," said Walt Moore's voice out of another room. Minutes passed, and then Walt Moore himself came into the kitchen: tall, white-haired, and freshly shaved, wrapped in a bathrobe over worn pajamas. "Good morning, Sennie," he said. "So what's the occasion?"

"Well, first of all, the *Abigail Prinn*'s going to get to Buffalo today or maybe tomorrow, and my dad and Mr. Shray will be coming up here as soon as they can." She called the details to mind. "Two rooms for three nights."

"Let me get that written down." He went out of the room, came back a minute later. "It'll be great to see them. Is your other message more good news?"

"I'm not sure," Asenath admitted, and described Cassie's sudden appearance atop Elk Hill and the way she had answered Betty Hale's questions.

"Odd," said Walt. "Well, I'll have someone ride up to Emeryville in a couple of hours and see if they know anything. Tell Betty thank you for the heads up."

With that errand taken care of, she went back out onto Chorazin's main street, a gravel road with a few businesses on it and maybe thirty houses. An air of destitution and decadence hovered over the town, but Asenath knew how carefully that was fostered by the inhabitants, part of the camouflage that kept them as safe as the worshipers of the Great Old Ones could be in that troubled age. Bleat of goats and cluck of chickens from behind the houses blended with human and half-human voices, telling her that all was well on an ordinary morning.

Halfway to Betty's house, recalling another errand, she veered to one side of the street, ducked between two houses, wished the goats in the back yard a cheerful good morning, and ducked through another kitchen door to find another familiar face turning toward her. "Good morning, Mrs. Hale."

"Why, good morning, Sennie," said Janey Hale. She was a cousin of Betty's and looked it, though her body was a little rounder, her hair not quite so gray. Her cotton dress and apron showed plenty of wear. "What can I do for you?"

"I got some news through the moon's rays last night," said Asenath. "My dad and Mr. Shray should be at Buffalo today or tomorrow, and they'll be coming straight here."

Janey nodded "I thought it was getting on time for that. You'd best let Robin know." She turned, called through the open door into the parlor: "Seth? Do you know where Robin is?"

"I'll get him, Mom," said a boy's voice in return.

"Tell him not to worry about his shape," Asenath called after him. "It's just me."

A few minutes passed while Asenath and Janey Hale talked about the weather, and then two boys came into the kitchen. Seth was twelve and had the dark straight hair and olive skin of the Chorazin folk. Robin, fifteen, had hair that was not so much blond as colorless, pale eyes, a thin face with high cheekbones. He didn't always look like that, and it bothered Asenath a little that he'd taken the trouble to put on a human shape.

Both the boys were barefoot and wore overalls with no shirts—sensible, that, with another hot August day beginning to gather strength. Asenath remembered the days when she'd been young enough not to have to bother with tops in really hot weather, and missed that freedom. She pushed the thought out of her mind, passed on her message. Seth grinned, but Robin looked at the floor, ambivalence written on his face. Janey, without a word, went over and hugged him, and he gave her a troubled look, hugged her back.

"Dad says I can go with the wagon down to Buffalo this year," Seth said to Asenath, distracting her. She turned toward him and said something more or less encouraging in response, but as soon as she could she extracted herself from the kitchen, ducked back out to the bare dirt street, and finished her journey.

CHAPTER 2

THE CITY OF THE BRIDGES

She came in the kitchen door of Betty Hale's house a few minutes later to find Betty at the woodstove and Cassie sitting at the table, her shoulders hunched and her hands folded in her lap. Betty was busy frying grated potatoes and sausage in a big cast iron pan. Asenath greeted them both, pulled her apron off a peg on one wall, put it on and went to help with breakfast.

Cassie watched both of them as though she'd never seen anyone cook a meal before. She thanked them both in a small scared voice when the meal was served, waited while they said grace—silently, since she was an outsider and shouldn't hear the names of the Great Old Ones spoken aloud—and ate slowly, a little at a time. By the time she'd finished the meal she looked a little less haggard, but she'd begun to blink and rub her eyes.

"Sleep will do her good," Betty said, once they'd gotten her settled on Asenath's bed with a quilt thrown over her, and Rachel had curled up a little resentfully on a pillow in a closet—kyrrmis were another thing outsiders couldn't be allowed to learn about. "She's surely had some kind of shock, enough to shake her wits a little. Some rest, some herbs, a spell or two, and she'll be better." With a little shrug: "If that's what the matter is."

Asenath gave her teacher a long wary look. "And if it's not?"

"Then we'll have to see." Betty met her gaze. After a moment: "Tell me this. Do you think the brambles on Elk Hill would let a stray child from outside wander up to the top?"

"No, but—" Asenath began, and then stopped.

"Exactly," said Betty. Neither of them had to say anything else. Another secret, far more dangerous to reveal to outsiders than any other, hung unspoken in the air between them: a strange power Asenath had received from the goddess she worshiped. A witch of centuries-old legend had possessed it before her, but it had been lost even more completely than kyrrmis and their powers over dream, and they both knew of a certain organization that would kill and kill again if its members found out that the power had been recovered.

The Radiance. The name hovered unspoken in the silence between them.

They busied themselves with the ordinary tasks of the day after that: fashioning amulets of protection and blessing for a baby who'd be born within the month, starting work on an herbal salve, and reviewing the things that Asenath had learned that summer, since she would be leaving for home within days. When Cassie woke up and came tentatively out of the bedroom they turned the conversation smoothly away from magic and went back to work on the salve. Betty asked the girl if she'd like to help by picking leaves off stems of dried herbs, and got a sudden luminous smile in response; once she understood what was needed, Cassie turned all her attention to it, and blushed when Betty praised her for the work.

Later in the day, Betty went out for a while: to Walt Moore's, Asenath guessed, to find out if the messenger he'd sent up to Emeryville had learned anything about a missing girl. While they waited, Asenath invited Cassie to come with her to the back yard to take care of the goats and chickens. The girl met the animals with astonished delight—as though she's never seen a hen before, Asenath thought, baffled—and had no idea what to do with them, but followed Asenath's instructions and helped where she could.

Betty was back by the time they hauled two pails of milk into the kitchen. "No luck," she said to Asenath, and to Cassie: "Why don't you sit down and tell me a little more about the house where you lived with your stepfather. Mr. Moore at the motel here sent some people to find it but they couldn't be sure where to look."

Cassie nodded after a moment, took the proffered seat, and said, "If they can't find it, maybe someone can take me back to Yian instead."

Asenath sent a quick astonished glance at Betty, who simply regarded the girl for a long moment and then asked, "What did you say, child?"

Cassie stared at her. In a small voice: "I—I said—maybe I can go back to Yian."

"You've been there."

The girl nodded, and Betty blinked and considered her for a long moment before saying, "Why don't you tell me what you know about Yian?"

She managed an unsteady smile. "It's so pretty there." When Betty gestured for her to go on: "All green gardens and great spreading trees and bridges of white stone and hanging lamps everywhere like stars, and—and the air smells like flowers and there are always silver bells chiming, and there are birds that are bright red and happy and birds that are gray and rose and very wise, and the white mountain off in the distance, tall and silent and old. I could see it from the garden where I played."

By that point Betty was nodding slowly. All at once Cassie seemed to notice that, and her eyes went round and teary. "You know about Yian! Can you tell me how to go back there? Oh, please tell me you've been there and you'll take me home!"

"Yes, I know about Yian," said Betty, "though I've never been there, nor ever thought to be. As for getting you home, that's no easy thing, but I'll see what I can do."

Cassie blinked back tears and smiled, a little less unsteadily. "Thank you."

* * *

"Yian-Ho," Bill Downey said. The senior initiate of Chorazin's Starry Wisdom church, he was plump and bald, and looked much less dangerous than he was. His parlor, where he sat with Asenath and Betty Hale that evening, had plain furniture, old family photos in frames on the walls, and a small shelf in one corner full of strange old books that sorcerers of olden times had sought and died for. "The city of a thousand bridges and ten thousand lamps, beneath a nameless white mountain, where a single afternoon stretches for a year or more. To travel there you have to cross seven oceans and the great river that's longer than from the earth to the moon." He sent a speculative glance toward Asenath. "Can you tell me what that means?"

"Of course," said Asenath, who'd encountered the last part of the description in the *Necronomicon*. "The seven oceans are the orbits of the seven planets that humans knew about before our telescopes got good enough to see the others, and the great river that's longer than from the earth to the moon is the Milky Way. But Yian can't actually be outside the galaxy—" She caught herself, met his glance with a puzzled one of her own. "Can it?"

A shake of the old man's head denied it. "There's plenty outside this one little galaxy, but we'll never know much of anything about it. No, you're halfway there."

She pondered that. After a moment: "It's not in the universe of matter."

"Good. Where is it?"

Then she knew. "The kingdom of Voor, the place where the light goes when it's put out and the water goes when the sun dries it up."

By way of answer Bill glanced at Betty, who allowed a smile and said, "I'll grant her this, she's not a bit behind on her studies."

"So I see," said Bill. To Asenath: "Yian is one of the ways the kingdom of Voor shows itself to humans, when it shows itself at all. To us, it's the realm of the unseen, but to the people who dwell there, our world and all the worlds of the greater Earth belong to the unseen."

"Eibon talked about that," Asenath ventured. "He said it was outside time and space."

"He did indeed."

"But—" Asenath paused, tried to put her thoughts in order. "How could someone like Cassie end up there? I don't think she knows any sorcery at all."

"Someone else could have sent her there," said Betty. "Maybe her stepfather knows some of the old lore. Or one of the powers of the kingdom of Voor could have taken her. Or one of the Great Old Ones could have done it for some reason we'll never know." With a little curt shrug: "The question on my mind is what are we going to do with her now that she's here."

"Might be something in the old lore," said Bill. "I'll see what I can find, and ask the other initiates to take a look. In the meantime, why, treat her the way we'd treat any lost child."

After a little more discussion and a little gossip, Betty and Asenath said their goodbyes and headed out into the cool damp air of a summer evening. The shadow of Elk Hill stretched blue and still across the little town. Tang of fried onions drifted from the chimney of the nameless bar and grill across from the motel, and made Asenath's mouth water. Back in Betty's kitchen, it didn't take long for similiar scents to fill the air, and an hour or so later they and Cassie sat down to a dinner of chicken, biscuits, and cooked greens. Cassie said almost nothing until the meal was done and a comfortable silence opened up. Then, visibly gathering up her courage, she asked, "Is there a place called Cardinal Woods?"

That got her startled looks from both the others. "Why, I don't know," said Betty. "I can ask around and find out. Why?"

"You were about to ask me about my stepfather's house," said Cassie, "and then I said what I did about Yian. But I thought and thought after you went, and I'm sure my stepfather said once that the woods around us were called Cardinal Woods."

"Cardinal Woods," Betty repeated thoughtfully. "No, I'm sure I haven't heard of it, but we'll find someone who has."

That night, after she'd fed chicken and greens to Rachel, said her prayers, settled down to sleep in the waking world and woke in the lands of dream, Asenath went further west along the shore of the Twilight Sea with the Hills of Hap rising to her left. Sometimes you could ask the Dreamlands a question and have it give you an answer, she'd learned that by experience and then read about it in the pages of the *Book of Eibon*. Thinking about Cassie's baffling arrival, she decided to try it that night. She paused on the beach trail, raised her arms, spoke three words in a language that had been old when the ancestors of humans first clambered awkwardly down from the trees, and then realized she wasn't sure what question to ask. Practical concerns carried the day, and she said aloud, "Is there a place in the waking world called Cardinal Woods?"

Nothing happened immediately in response, but Asenath was used to that. She started walking again, reached up to rub Rachel under the chin where she most liked it, and was still doing that when three small shapes of brilliant red shot one by one through the air in front of her, out from the trees to her left and then back into them. It took her one moment to realize that they were birds, and another to recognize them as cardinals.

It was as clear a yes as the Dreamlands had ever given her. She pondered that as she journeyed on toward Ogrothan.

* * *

Late the next afternoon, as Asenath and Cassie were taking care of the goats and chickens, low indistinct sounds from somewhere off to the south gradually turned into the plodding of horses' hooves and the crunch of tires on the gravel road. Voices rose in response, and it took a sustained effort for Asenath to keep from abandoning Cassie and the livestock and hurrying to see. Finally, though, as every sound but the voices died away, they got the second nanny milked and hauled the pails into the kitchen, and Betty Hale called Cassie over to help take care of the milk and made a gesture with her head at Asenath: get out there.

Asenath didn't have to be told twice, and moments later pelted down the walk in front of Betty's house. There in the parking lot beside the Elk Hill Motor Hotel was an ungainly contraption of wood and metal, the big truck tires on its six wheels revealing part of its lineage, the four patient draft horses being freed from their harnesses in front displaying another part. It had square sides rising up nearly as high as you could go and still get under the bridge at Fox Junction ten miles south of Chorazin, and a crew of older boys was busy unloading bags and boxes and metal buckets from inside. Asenath had to get most of the way there before she saw, off past a stack of cargo, Walt Moore talking with—

"Dad!" she shouted, and followed it up by breaking into a sprint and flinging herself at him. Three months hadn't changed him noticeably in her eyes: solidly built, with broad shoulders and sandy hair touched with gray, and a square clean-shaven face that looked solemn when he wasn't laughing. He laughed as he caught her, spun around to break her momentum, plopped her back down onto her feet. He and Walt picked up the conversation as though nothing had interrupted it, and Asenath stood beside her father, beaming at no one in particular, until they had finished sharing a first round of news.

"Hi, kiddo," he said to her then. "You look like you're doing well."

"I've had a really good time," she said, "but I missed you and Mom and Barney and, well, everybody. Are they all okay?"

"Everyone's fine," he reassured her. "I'll tell you all the news this evening."

Asenath smiled up at him and then stepped back, for plenty of other people waited to greet her father. As Bill Downey came up to do that, she turned, saw another familiar face, went over to him. "Hi, Mr. Shray."

"Hi, Sennie." Larry Shray, short and muscular, had been a presence in her life since long before her first memories. His real name was Shray Lharep, Asenath knew, and she also knew enough of Tchosi, the Tcho-Tcho language, to say to him, "*Shob Nekhrang dza'yakh.*"*

That got her a grin. "*A dza'yimh,*"† he replied. Then: "She has, too. The baby came on July twelfth—she's fine and so is Patty." Then, before she could respond with anything but a delighted noise, he looked past her. "Hi, Robin. I've got some messages for you from your dad and Belinda."

"I want to hear all about the baby," Asenath told him. "Tonight, okay?" Then, matching his grin with hers, she moved back toward her father, found him surrounded by a knot of Chorazin folk, and turned to look at Robin instead.

He was still wearing nothing but a pair of well-worn overalls, and that stirred old uncomfortable memories. The two of them had known each other practically from the cradle, they'd spent summers together at Kingsport further back than she could recall, and once he'd moved to Arkham with his father and stepmother—he'd been ten then and she'd been eleven—they'd talked and run and played together constantly, and the fact that he was a boy and she was a girl meant no more to either of them than the fact that she had one shape and he could take many. Years passed, though, and eventually

---

* "May the Black Goat of the Woods bless you."
† "And you also."

the differences couldn't be ignored any longer. She hated that, hated the awkwardness the changes in their bodies had put between them.

That was on her mind now and again over the hours that followed, as the two of them helped with the impromptu potluck in the Starry Wisdom church basement that celebrated the arrival of honored guests with a wagon full of goods from distant Arkham. She had plenty of other things to occupy her attention though: a summer's worth of news from her father and Larry Shray, to begin with, and the first round of thank-yous and partings with the people in Chorazin, since she'd be leaving with her father for the trip back to Arkham.

Later, too, as the potluck wound down, Betty caught Asenath's gaze, motioned for her to follow, went to talk to her father briefly, and then led the two of them upstairs into the dimly lit worship hall. She wanted to talk to him about Cassie—no surprises there, Asenath thought, for her father was a scholar as well as a Starry Wisdom initiate, and had access to two libraries full of rare volumes no one in Chorazin had ever seen. Owen listened to Betty's account of the girl's appearance and then to Asenath's, nodding slowly.

"The Cardinal Woods," he said when they'd finished. "That was what she said?" When Betty confirmed it: "That's just north of the Adirondacks, not far from the St. Lawrence. We'll be sailing right past it on the way home." He glanced at her, considering. "If you think she might have come from there, you know, she could come with us. If we can't find her stepfather there, we can certainly give her a home in Arkham and try something else."

"That might be best," Betty said after a moment. "If I was her stepfather I know I'd be frantic by now, and she surely misses him."

* * *

When Betty raised the prospect the next morning, Cassie burst
into tears, thanked her, and agreed at once. By then the girl
had had her hair combed out and washed, and the Chorazin
folk had found her some spare clothes and a pair of shoes with
soles salvaged from old tires, the same as everyone in the little
village wore when they bothered with shoes at all. Asenath
had wondered what she'd think of Chorazin clothing; outsiders dressed differently, and used words like "old-fashioned"
for the sort of good sensible homespun clothes that Asenath
had grown up wearing. Still, Cassie received each of the things
she was given with tearful thanks, and treated bathing and
combing the way she'd watched Betty and Asenath cooking,
as though she was witnessing strange rites never seen before.
Asenath watched it all and wondered.

With the end of another summer in Chorazin and the trip
back home to Arkham imminent, she had no shortage of goodbyes to say and friends to thank for various favors and lessons.
She spent one evening in the Starry Wisdom church making a
thank-offering in the sanctuary—as a first-degree initiate she
couldn't go into the sanctuary alone, but Betty accompanied her,
and sat impassively in one of the seven tall chairs while Asenath
lit the incense, chanted the words, and let a single drop of blood
fall from a pricked finger onto the smoke-colored crystal in its
open golden box on the altar. The sudden flash of crimson light
as the blood dissolved into the kingdom of Voor cheered her.

The next morning, before the sun was up, she went to the
hidden shrine of Yhoundeh the elk goddess, low on the southern flank of Elk Hill, to kneel there and pour out her thanks.
Chorazin and its people were Yhoundeh's, bound together
through long bitter years of shared trouble and grief and final
release. More than once during her summers at the village,
Asenath had seen the goddess: in dreams, as a winged elk or
a tall slender woman with elk's antlers, at whom one should
never look directly; in the waking world, as the great spectral
shape of an elk against the sky, in a county where no elk had

been seen for more than a century, and once during a midnight vigil as a vast presence with many tentacles and many eyes looming over Elk Hill, with the brighter stars just faintly visible through her form. She was the older half-sister of Phauz the cat goddess, a daughter of the Black Goat of the Woods by the cold god Ithaqua, and she was one of the Great Old Ones Asenath had prayed to since she'd gotten old enough to talk. Outsiders found the Great Old Ones terrifying, she knew that in the same abstract sense that she knew about Yuggoth and the Ghooric Zone, but she'd never been able to understand why.

Most of the time that didn't go into goodbyes and thank-yous went into hard work, for the ship that sailed twice a year from Arkham to Buffalo and back took plenty of goods both ways, and Chorazin's contributions to the trade had to be packed, sealed, protected with spells, and loaded aboard the big ramshackle wagon in the motel parking lot. Finally, late in the afternoon before the trip to Buffalo, the last packages were tied in place, tarps tied over them, and an enchantment woven over that—the last of those by Betty, with Asenath's enthusiastic help. One more potluck in the church basement, one last round of tearful farewells, and then an hour sitting with Betty Hale at the kitchen table over two cups of steaming tea: Cassie was already asleep and so they could talk freely about what Asenath had learned that summer, what she would be studying in Arkham from fall through to spring, and what Betty hoped to teach her once she came back to Chorazin the next year.

A few hours of dreamless sleep, a cold breakfast before first light, and she and Cassie went out to the motel parking lot to meet the others. Robin was there already, and so was Seth Hale, who was grinning from ear to ear. Seth still had battered overalls on, though he'd compromised to the extent of tire-soled cloth shoes and a loose shirt with short sleeves. Robin had put on Arkham clothes, though, trousers, a shirt with buttons, and leather shoes, and had a long brown instrument bag slung over one shoulder for the mountain dulcimer he played whenever he had free time. His eyes were red and he didn't say much. He'd been born and died and then been reborn, and still remembered enough of his short first life that it hurt to leave his first mother at each summer's end; knowing that, Asenath wished she could go over and give him a hug, the way she'd done in past years.

The others came to join them: her father, Larry Shray, and three people from Chorazin, Tom Eagle and Sue and Micah Moore, leading the draft horses. The sky brightened slowly in the east as harness jingled and clattered, and the horses made whickering noises. Asenath wished she could have Rachel with her, but they'd be among outsiders the whole way, to say nothing of Cassie's presence. The kyrrmi would be staying with Betty until Asenath used the power she dared not name to fetch her home again.

"Everything ready?" Tom Eagle said. "Good." To the lead horse: "Come on, Sally. Time to get a move on." The horses stamped and started forward and the wagon began to roll. Above them, thin streamers of mist coiled around the brambles of Elk Hill.

* * *

The main route west to Buffalo, Highway 20, hadn't been fit to travel on for two years. One too many overpasses had come crashing down after years of neglect, and it was easier to head south and then west on county roads than it was to get scores of people and draft horses together to haul the big gray masses of concrete out of the way. Since no one was in a hurry, the trip was pleasant enough: two days walking beside or behind the wagon, stopping every couple of hours to give the horses rest and water, with trees to shade the way more often than not until they got into what was left of the Buffalo suburbs. For Asenath and Robin, it was a familiar trip; for Seth, it was an adventure; Cassie watched everything with wide eyes but stayed close to Asenath and followed her lead.

They stopped for the night at a Tcho-Tcho farm between Cowlesville and Marilla and slept out under the stars. Waking up when the first gray dawn was stirring, Asenath got out from inside her blanket roll, shook out the clothes she'd slept in, spotted her father and Tom Eagle getting the campfire going again, made sure Cassie was still asleep, and then went over to where Robin was sleeping and sat down beside his blanketed form. "Wake up, sleepyhead," she said. "You ought to look human before Cassie sees you."

The caution wasn't exaggerated. The shape underneath the blanket roll had nothing even remotely human about it, and what appeared blearily from the open end was not a head but a single eye on a stalk and a half dozen ropy tentacles. Those stretched and flowed, joined several more tentacles, and turned into Robin's head. "Thanks," he said.

"Sure thing." She got up, went to the campfire to warm herself. Seeing Robin in his primary form, the one he returned to when he was asleep or too tired to hold another, didn't trouble her at all. If anything, it reminded her of earlier and less complicated days, when he'd had to make a serious effort to hold a human shape for more than a few hours. It was just an ordinary thing, she thought, if you knew about the Great Old Ones and their habit of mating with humans, but of course outsiders couldn't be expected to see it that way.

They were on the road again before the sun had finished clearing the hills in the east. Heavy rains the winter before had washed out the road further on, so they had to veer southward again and then turn west to reach Interstate 90 a little past Hamburg. That was still passable—the interstates, Asenath thought she remembered, still got some maintenance long after most other roads were handed over to the weather—and the wagon took the onramp up to the broad gray paving and headed north at a walking pace.

Until that point the only people they'd met were farmers, some of them Tcho-Tchos, others local people whose families had been in that part of New York State for generations and weren't going to leave no matter how hard times got or how gaudy the promises of jobs out west might get, all of them used to makeshift wagons rumbling toward Buffalo or away from it. On the interstate, though, a few cars and trucks passed them by, most of them battered and dusty. The wagon stayed on the outside lane and pulled over onto the shoulder when the horses needed a rest. The cars and trucks stayed close to the median, announcing their coming with the low irritated grumble of engines making do with low-quality fuel, rattling past at a speed Asenath thought was a good deal slower than the cars of her childhood had gone, vanishing again in the distance before or behind.

They were maybe halfway to Buffalo when something a little different came rumbling up out of the distance behind them. Seth Hale, who had the best eyes in the group, stared back at it when it wasn't much more than a dot, and scrambled up onto the wagon. "Mama Black Goat and *all* her kids!" he said, which was as close as a Chorazin boy his age could come to swearing and get away with it. "It's *purple*."

It was. The horses were looking tired, and so Tom Eagle guided them over onto the shoulder, brought them and the wagon to a gradual stop, and started freeing them from their harnesses so they could rest and drink. Asenath spared a glance away from the oncoming vehicle, noted with alarm that her father had quietly gone to the end of the wagon where a few guns had been tucked for emergency use. She turned, caught Robin's gaze, and motioned with her head; he looked that way, nodded quickly; she went to Cassie and led her over to the road's edge, where they could shelter behind the wagon if shots were fired, and Robin did the same with Seth. Once they were out of harm's way, Asenath twined her fingers together and murmured the words of a protective spell. Voor flowed around her, reassuring.

The vehicle rumbled closer. It closed the distance over the next few minutes, and then wheezed and rattled to a halt close by. It wasn't a truck, though it took Asenath a little while to sort through the vehicles she'd seen in girlhood and give a name to it, and by then Sue Moore laughed in delight and said, "A tour bus? Seriously? Owen, any idea who Orichalc might be?" She gestured at the side of the bus, where that word was painted in stark white over purple.

"Yes, I do," Owen said, grinning. "If it's the same band."

The door of the bus clanked and lurched open, and a woman in her thirties clattered down the steps. Looking around the front of the wagon, Asenath blinked in surprise—she'd heard that outsiders dyed their hair, but nobody had seen fit to mention that some dyed it the same bright purple color as the side of the bus.

Owen walked over toward the bus, making sure that both his hands were in sight, and said, "Good afternoon. You're Molly Wolejko, aren't you?"

That got him a grin. "Guilty as charged. I'm glad someone still remembers us on this end of the continent."

"I saw you perform when I was in grad school," said Owen. "Heading for Buffalo?"

"Yeah, we'll be playing there if we can find a venue. Do you know if the road's open all the way into town?"

"It was a week ago. If you're going downtown or to the harbor, take the I-180 exit."

"Great. Give me half a sec." She went back up the stair into the bus, returned with a sheaf of printed tickets the same color as her hair. "Comp tickets," she said. "Don't know where it'll be, but you're all invited." Owen thanked her, she grinned and trotted back aboard the bus. The door clanked shut, the bus grumbled to itself and lurched into motion, and a few minutes later it was a receding black dot on the freeway ahead.

Once it was well ahead, Asenath left the shelter of the wagon. "Dad," she said tentatively, "what was that about?"

Owen turned toward her with a reminiscent grin. "Before your time, kiddo, music groups used to travel all over the country in buses like that, going from one gig to another. I had no idea any of them were still on the road. But Orichalc—they used to have quite a reputation."

"Orichalc," she repeated. "Like orichalcum—the Atlantean metal."

"Yeah. It's a joke, more or less. There's a kind of music called metal, and that's what Orichalc plays, but they play weird metal."

Asenath gave him a dubious look, but nodded. The idea of "metal music" made her think of pots and pans clanking in the sink and blacksmiths hard at work, but she guessed that those probably weren't what it sounded like. "Do you think I'd like it?"

"We'll find out." He gestured with the tickets. "They put on a really good show twenty years ago, and we ought to be able to spare an evening before the *Abigail Prinn*'s loaded."

CHAPTER 3

THE DANCE OF THE KNIFE

A fternoon was well under way before the wagon finally rumbled to a halt next to another, similar wagon, just as heavily laden, on a long spit of industrial brownland that jutted into Buffalo's outer harbor. The *Abigail Prinn*, a sturdy two-masted schooner, waited there for her cargo. Asenath had been aboard her more than a dozen times—that same ship had brought her from Arkham to Buffalo at summer's beginning—and she greeted the purser and the crew cheerfully, got most of her gear stowed in the tiny cabin amidships where she'd be sleeping on the voyage, and then headed back on deck.

After that, as burly longshoremen hauled cargo aboard and stowed it belowdecks, she went with her father and the others back the way they'd come, across the harbor canal and the winding Buffalo River to a neighborhood she knew nearly as well as she knew Chorazin. It was one of the two main Tcho-Tcho neighborhoods in Buffalo, a patchwork of old houses and older industrial buildings of red brick, some of the latter falling down and others put to new purposes. Brightly painted signs in English and Tchosi vied with one another for Asenath's attention and a very few cars drove by as she picked her way along broken sidewalks to a familiar corner. From there, she, her father, Cassie, and Larry Shray headed to a big blue house halfway up the next block, as they always did, while Robin, Seth, and the others went another way.

At the door of the blue house she had old friends to greet: Shray Khorep, the patriarch of the family; Larry's older sister and her husband—they went by Jill and Ken, though their real names were Nzelhe and Kyan; their six children, the oldest ten, the youngest still cradled in her mother's arms; Larry's wife Patty, who had brown hair and a pleasant round face, and stood taller than her in-laws; and Larry and Patty's daughters, four-year-old Tammy and month-old Jane. Once everyone was indoors and a few night's worth of luggage found its way to guest rooms upstairs, Asenath and Cassie came back downstairs to join the others. Cushions on the floor around a low rectangular table, tea and conversation, the social rituals of an ancient culture Asenath had grown up with: it was comforting in its familiarity, an anchor in a changing world.

One face she'd expected to see was missing, though. There were customs to follow and taboos to watch out for, and so she had to wait until a member of the family mentioned the name before saying, "So how's Evan doing?"

"Right at the moment?" Patty Shray beamed. "He's probably having a pretty rough time of it. He's been at the *pauw* since something like three this morning." She turned to her husband. "He'll be so happy that you were able to make it back in time."

"Makes two of us," said Larry. To Asenath: "Master Nhau—you remember him, right?" She nodded enthusiastically, and he went on. "He got here a week ago from Cleveland. No warning, he just showed up the way he did that time in Arkham, watched some practices, taught some classes, and then suddenly announced that he was going to do a *dzil shao*, a full formal examination. So that's where Evan is."

"Tonight's the night?" Owen asked.

Patty nodded. "For the boys, yes, six o'clock tonight. You two can certainly come if you like. I know Evan would love to see you there."

Owen glanced at his daughter, who grinned. "Wouldn't miss it for the world," he said.

Quarter to six that evening accordingly brought Asenath with her father, Larry, Patty, and Khorep to one of the old brick commercial buildings in the neighborhood, where a long narrow stair led up to the third floor. At the top, the door had a sign over it in Tchosi; Asenath knew only a few dozen words in that language, but recognized *pauw*, "training hall." Inside, twenty or so boys in dark red trousers and coats moved through something that looked like a dance if you didn't pay attention to the sudden movements of fists and feet. Nearly all of them had the Asian features, black hair, and stocky build of the Tcho-Tchos, but in among them was a tall boy with brown hair and a round smiling face Asenath recognized at first glance: Evan Shray. They were warming up, Asenath knew, and followed her father and the others over to one side of the room, where family members and friends sat and watched. She settled comfortably on a flat red cushion, folded her legs up neatly beneath her, and watched with interest.

Arkham had its own school of *khrang tayeng*, the martial art of the Tcho-Tcho men's side; Tcho-Tcho women had their own way of fighting, and Asenath had learned a good deal of it growing up, but she'd also visited the *pauw* in Arkham often enough to know what was going on in front of her. Once the boys had finished warming up, a thin and wrinkled old man in the same red garments came out from somewhere in back; he bowed to the boys, they bowed to him, and then paired up and began working through the formal patterns of attack and defense. After a while, at the old man's signal, they changed partners and sparred with one another in quick flurries of punches and kicks. Another signal had them change partners again and repeat the process with wooden versions of the big leaf-bladed knives that Tcho-Tcho men carried.

Another signal from the old man stopped the sparring. The boys bowed to the old man and the watchers, and went to the other side of the room to sit on the floor. A silence, and then the old man called out two names and the Tchosi name of a combat form. Two boys stood, bowed to him and then to each other, and began.

This was the crucial part of the *dzil shao*, Asenath knew. Those students who'd shown that they were ready for formal testing would be set a form that was at the furthest edge of their skills, and if they completed it flawlessly, they would advance to a higher rank. The boys closed on each other in a flurry of punches and kicks. They finished, bowed, went back to their places; the master called two more and assigned them a more challenging form. Another pair followed, and another. Asenath glanced now and then from the boys to Master Nhau, whose eyes missed nothing and revealed nothing.

Another pair completed a complex form full of high kicks, bowed, and returned to their places. "Shray Yevanh," the old man said then. The brown-haired boy stood and bowed. Asenath waited for another name to be called. Instead, the old man rose smoothly to his feet and stepped out onto the floor of the *pauw*. He bowed to Evan, then drew a Tcho-Tcho knife—steel, not wood—from a sheath in his sash, and raised it overhead in one hand, point up.

* * *

That was when Asenath realized what was happening, and her hand went to her mouth. *Nga khatun*, the knife-throwing drill, was one of *khrang tayeng*'s signature practices. The big leaf-bladed knife, sharp enough to shave with, could be thrown straight like a spear or with a flip of the wrist to make it turn in flight, and a good eye and quick reflexes made it possible to dodge the blade and catch the hilt as it went by. Students of *khrang tayeng* practiced it by the hour, first with wooden knives, then with blunt steel, then with sharp blades, for nothing else trained hand and eye so precisely, and nothing else brought the cold reality of combat so close. To do it with a sharp knife with a master of *khrang tayeng* was something beyond that, a rite of passage that she had heard of but never seen.

A moment of perfect stillness passed, and then the teacher threw the knife at Evan. The boy twisted out of the way, caught the hilt, held the knife aloft, and threw it back. Master Nhau caught it easily, paused, and threw it again. Asenath's heart was in her throat as the knife flashed back and forth between teacher and pupil.

When the boy had caught the knife by the hilt eight times without injury or error, the old man raised his right hand, palm out, stopping the exchange. Evan held the knife point up, waiting. The old man bowed to him—Asenath could hear the sudden delighted murmurs to either side of her—and then slid the sheath out of his sash and tossed it to Evan, who caught it with his other hand. The old man turned, bowed wordlessly to Shray Khorep, who rose with a grace most eighty-year-olds couldn't manage, bowed to the teacher and the boy, helped Evan place the sheathed knife in his sash, and tied a red cord around his left arm in an intricate pattern.

All that was in perfect silence, but once the cord was tied, Khorep led his grandson over to the other watchers, and everyone in the *pauw* applauded—that American habit, at least, had found a place in *khrang tayeng*. The boy, eyes shining, exchanged bows with Larry, and then Larry flung his arms around his stepson and said, "Evan, that was great. You've done your old man proud." Patty simply hugged him and murmured something in his ear that made Evan turn pink. He was still blushing when he bowed to Asenath, and she made him turn a little pinker by making her own bow deeper than usual as a sign of respect.

He went back to sit among the other students, and the teacher of the Buffalo *pauw*—a stocky middle-aged man whose movements were deft as a cat's—came out from a back room with certificates and a rolled scroll. One after another, the students who'd earned new ranks went to the master's end of the room, exchanged bows, waited for their certificates to be signed, and then went to join their families and friends and be congratulated. Evan was the last to go up, and Khorep rose when he did and gestured for the rest of them to follow. Asenath gave the old man an uncertain look, but Patty turned to her and Owen and motioned with her head: come on.

Asenath bowed to Master Nhau with the others, watched as the old man unrolled the scroll. It had a long list of Tcho-Tcho names on it in the intricate Tchosi script, giving the lineage of Evan's teachers. At the bottom the old man wrote Evan's name in Tchosi, then extracted an intricately carved piece of stone from inside his jacket—a stone seal or chop, its bottom end stained a dull red. That end went down onto a vermilion ink pad and then onto the scroll, leaving a square red imprint with intricate flowing glyphs on it. If they were Tchosi, Asenath thought, they didn't look like any version of the language she'd ever seen.

The scroll had to stay open a few minutes for the ink to dry, but that simply meant that Evan had time to field another round of congratulations from his family and his fellow students, before he went to a back room to change into street clothes. By the time he reappeared, a bag of martial arts gear over one shoulder, the *pauw* was mostly empty. Asenath waited while Evan and his stepfather rolled the scroll carefully and tied it shut, then followed the others down the stair.

They stopped at the big blue house just long enough to pick up Jill, Ken, their children, Evan's two half-sisters, and Cassie, who seemed to have shed some of her fearfulness. From there they went a few blocks the other direction to another fixture of Asenath's memories: the Sarkomand Restaurant, where Larry's uncle Gyoreng served up the best Tcho-Tcho food this side of the plateau of Leng. After the appetizers appeared, Gyoreng came out from the kitchen to talk with Evan. "*Yeng dakh*, and you only fifteen?" the old man said, beaming, and Asenath knew she hadn't been mistaken; that rank was something like a black belt in other martial arts, a rank few Tcho-Tcho boys earned before adulthood if they reached it at all. She'd seen how relentlessly Evan had trained in the Arkham *pauw*, but even so it was a little dizzying to hear the adult Tcho-Tchos talk about the boy's future as a teacher and lineage-holder of *khrang tayeng*.

All the while, as Asenath took a little of her favorite dishes and listened to the conversation while saying little, her thoughts veered toward and away from something she could not have named if she'd wanted to. She only shook it off when dinner finally ended and she headed with the others back to the Shrays' house. The little attic room where she'd stayed so many nights before was as welcoming as always, and she prayed to Phauz and got into her nightgown and slipped into the world of dreams.

Rachel met her in the *between* place, a place she'd learned how to pass into between falling asleep and reaching the top of the seventy steps that led to the cavern of flame, and an instant later they were by the shores of the Twilight Sea.

That night, while her body slept in Buffalo, she followed the trail toward Ogrothan through the Hills of Hap. Her thoughts kept straying away from the dream, though, sometimes toward Robin, sometimes toward Evan, and she finished the night's journey only a little closer to her destination. When Rachel sent a questioning chirr her way, she shrugged and said, "I don't know. I'm just feeling a little grumpy tonight, that's all."

She woke up late in a bad mood, and had to struggle to keep her mind on her morning prayers and meditations. When she went downstairs for breakfast, though, her father grinned and gestured with one of the purple tickets he'd been given by the woman from the bus. "Up for a metal concert tonight?" he asked her. "I heard from Tom Eagle first thing this morning."

"Sure," she said, and wondered again whether she'd like metal music.

* * *

Afterward, she wasn't sure whether she liked it or not. She and her father left late that afternoon and wove their way through half-familiar neighborhoods to a big warehouse that, she gathered, had been turned into a music venue, with a lurid handpainted sign above the door and the grumbling of an unseen diesel generator sounding close by. The two of them started out walking alone, but by the time they got to the warehouse they were in the middle of a crowd, and had to stand in line for a while. Most of the other people in the line were her father's age or older, Asenath noted, and more than half of them wore old half-legible tee shirts that she guessed had something to do with the band, some with ORICHALC on them and some with odd images she recognized after a while as album covers from the vinyl records her father owned.

After a quarter hour or so, they got to the door, and Owen handed over two of the bright purple tickets to a tough-looking woman who stood just inside. From there they went on into a cavernous space with electric lamps overhead, a stage on one side, a big open space in the center for dancing, plenty of random chairs in unsteady rows, and over to one side a space full of little tables surrounded by chairs, with a bar and a counter for food service nearby. Owen led her to one of the tables, sat down more or less facing the stage; she took another chair with a decent view of the stage, sat, gave him a quizzical glance.

"We'll be here until late," Owen said. "What'll you have?"

She craned her neck to see the menu on the board above the food service counter, they discussed the options, and then Owen got up and headed for the line. The moment he was gone, a lean young man with greasy hair turned and moved purposefully in Asenath's direction. She spotted him, twisted her fingers together in an odd pattern and murmured the worlds of a witch's spell under her breath. The young man got a puzzled look on his face, and suddenly turned and hurried away, as though he'd just remembered an appointment somewhere else.

A quarter hour later, maybe, Owen came back with hamburgers, fries, a tall glass of very dark beer for himself and an even taller glass of lemonade for her. They tucked into the food while the last of the crowd arrived and a stocky man with a mane of unkempt black hair busied himself on the stage with microphone stands and wires. Finally the man went away, the lights in the warehouse went down, a cluster of spotlights came on, and Molly Wolejko came on stage, her purple hair ablaze in the light, a battered tee shirt and worn jeans for costume. The roar that rose from the crowd left Asenath unnerved, but a quick glance at her father found him grinning, so she turned back to the stage.

Others came onstage, one more woman and two men, and they all went to their instruments—guitar, bass, keyboard, and drums—as the crowd yelled. Molly, with the guitar, signaled to the drummer; a steady beat crackled out through loudspeakers the size of standing stones; a harsh fuzzy chord rang out from the guitar, then another, and the crowd hushed as Orichalc plunged into its first number. What it was about Asenath had no idea. Molly all but screamed the lyrics into the microphone and the music drowned out everything but the beat, but the music had its own fierce logic and Asenath, a little dazed, sat back and let herself listen.

By midway through the first number there were people dancing in the clear space in front of the stage; by the end of the third, the dance floor was crowded. Molly grinned and said something to the others on stage once that number was over, and after a pause a series of notes, far more melodic, rang out from Molly's guitar. The audience roared again, but there was a quality in the tumult of sound Asenath hadn't heard there before, something that tasted of longing for a vanished past. Over the roar of the crowd, the notes repeated, and then the band began playing in a more lyrical style while Molly sang about a journey to the east that was also a journey to the Moon, and circled back around to words about memory and grief.

They played a dozen pieces in all before the first set ended. Lights came up, the taut focus of the crowd dissolved into ebullient noise, and Asenath sipped lemonade and tried to think. Her father sent her a querying glance; she smiled back at him, and after a while the lights started to dim and the noise died down again.

Just before the house lights went black, for no reason that she could name, she happened to glance to her left, past her father. There, leaning back in a chair that must have been pulled away from one of the tables, sat a very tall man in a long black coat and a black broad-brimmed hat. His face was as long and lean as the rest of him, with a great hooked nose like a hawk's beak; eyes like polished black stones turned briefly from the stage to her; many rings glinted on his fingers, and as his gaze met hers, he raised one finger to his lips in a gesture for silence. An instant later the last light guttered out and Asenath could see nothing at all where the man had been, but for a long moment she stared, mouth open, at the blackness that had swallowed him.

It took an effort for her to pay attention to the music after that, though the yelling of the crowd, the driving beat of the music, and the fierce harmonies of voices and instruments made the effort a good deal easier. It seemed impossible that she could have seen what she'd seen, not least because it reminded her so much of a story she and her brother had begged their father to tell them hundreds of times, from before they were born, before he'd found his way to their mother and the people of the Great Old Ones, when he'd first met—

Nyarlathotep. The Crawling Chaos, the One in Black of countless whispered tales, he was the soul and mighty messenger of the Great Old Ones. One of Owen's first encounters with that legendary being had been in J.J.'s, Arkham's one music venue, where he'd seen the One in Black sitting not far from him, glanced away and then back, and seen no one there at all.

Another dozen songs rounded out the second set, and then the lights came back up. As Asenath more than half expected, the tall figure was no longer there, and neither was the chair. Her father noticed her expression and raised an eyebrow; she put on a smile in response—the crowd around them was loud enough that neither of them tried to speak. A few more sips of lemonade, the last of her glass, offered an additional distraction.

By the time the third set was well under way Asenath felt dazed by the raw intensity of the music, the bursts of rage and despair flung at things she'd never known, the sheer volume of the crowd's answering roar. The concert reached its end with cheers and whoops and applause that went on and on, and finally the lights came up and people began milling around, heading more or less toward the doors. Owen stayed seated until the crowd had thinned a little, then rose and started for the nearest door with Asenath alongside him.

Outside the air felt fresh and cool. Summer stars glittered above, blotted out here and there by the lightless towers of downtown Buffalo. Once the departing crowd had begun to thin, Owen glanced at her and said, "So what do you think, kiddo?"

"I'm not sure," she admitted. "Did you like it?"

That earned her a grin. "Yeah. They're even better than they were when I heard them. I think that was their first year on tour, and they were quite a bit younger then." With a little shrug: "So was I."

She gave him a dubious look, but he was silent for a while, his thoughts elsewhere.

* * *

The next day she got up late, and had just finished breakfasting on fried noodles and a tart peppery soup when Robin and Seth came over from the house where they were staying. They'd heard of the concert, and they both wanted to know all about it. Partway through the story that followed, Cassie came down the stairs from the room she'd been given, paused for an uncertain moment at the stair's foot, and then let the others encourage her to come over and sit with them. She sat on the sofa next to Asenath and sent a tentative smile her way; Asenath responded with a grin, and resumed the story.

Just as she finished—she'd described everything but Nyarlathotep's appearance, heeding the caution of that raised finger—the back door of the house clattered open. A moment later Evan came into the parlor, in shorts and a sweat-soaked tee shirt. Greetings followed, and then Evan headed up the stairs, saying with a grin, "Let me get hosed off and fit for company."

As his footfalls on the stair faded, Cassie turned to Asenath and asked, "What got him so wet?" Asenath blinked, realized that Cassie probably had never heard of *khrang tayeng*, and a few questions showed that she'd never heard of any other martial art either. She ended up describing the way he'd thrown and caught the knife at the *pauw* two nights before. That got a wide-eyed look from Cassie, but brought on a flurry of excited questions from Seth, who knew little more of *khrang tayeng* than the name. She was still fielding questions when Evan came back down the stairs, his hair wet but his clothes clean, and paused in the doorway.

"Can you help me out?" Asenath asked him as soon as she spotted him. "I've been trying to explain *nga khatun*."

Evan reddened. "It's just a drill you do if you practice *khrang tayeng*," he said. "No big deal. I want to hear about the concert you went to."

She opened her mouth, maybe to argue, maybe to repeat the story of the concert—afterwards, she could never remember which—when the front door opened and her father came in, fielding greetings from everyone in the parlor. "Can your friends spare you for a bit, Sennie?"

That got settled, and she trotted out the door with her father, wondering what he had in mind. He led the way down to the sidewalk and then said, "Up for an adventure?"

"Sure," she replied at once. "What kind?"

"That's the spirit," he said, grinning. "I went for a walk first thing this morning, ended up over by the place we were at last night, and ran into Molly Wolejko. She and the band are leaving tomorrow morning, and the road they're taking goes straight through Cardinal Springs, New York—right on the edge of the Cardinal Woods. People ride with them in exchange for gas money and groceries, and the *Abigail Prinn* won't be ready to sail for most of a week."

"So you want to go with them," she ventured.

"I want you and me and Cassie to go with them. We can see about finding Cassie's stepfather, and then go to Fernville on the St. Lawrence and wait for the *Abigail Prinn* there—but I want to make sure it's safe to go with them first, and that's witch's work."

Her face lit up. "Of course I can do that, Dad. I should see them, though."

"I told her you wanted to meet the band," Owen said. "Unless you've got something else planned for this morning—"

"Nope," she assured him. "Nothing at all."

A quarter hour later, they reached the big dilapidated warehouse where they'd seen the concert. Owen led the way around it, and there was the tour bus parked in back, with the door open, various hatches gaping wide, and the man she'd seen on stage before the concert doing something intricate with the engine in back. Owen paused, and Asenath gave him an uncertain look and then remembered what she was supposed to do. A surreptitious motion of two fingers and a few words murmured under her breath woke the necessary spell.

Moments later someone came out of the bus—a woman Asenath recognized after a moment as the keyboard player in the concert—and said, "Hi, Owen. Your daughter?"

"The one and only. Sennie, this is Kate Crosby. Kate, Asenath."

Kate was a lean muscular woman in her late thirties with short blonde hair, light skin, and features that would have been called rugged on a man's face. She shook Asenath's hand and said something polite, and Asenath came up with a suitable reply. All the attention she could spare was on the unseen world, the world of voor, where she could see the colors and shapes of the woman's personality and look for signs of treachery and hidden purposes. There was no trace of either, just a thick layer of brash good humor covering old insecurities and miseries.

"Let me introduce you to the others," Kate said, and turned. "Vern, got a minute?"

The black-haired man working on the engine glanced back over his shoulder, gave a monosyllabic grunt, went back to work. "Don't mind him," Kate said. "He's like that."

"I won't," said Asenath. "I promise." She meant it, too, for the glance and the grunt had been enough to let her glimpse the pattern of his personality and be certain she and her father had nothing to worry about.

Moments later the three of them clambered up the stair into the tour bus, and Kate introduced Asenath to the other members of the band: Molly Wolejko, who was sprawled in one of the swiveling chairs; Howie Fishbein, the drummer, who was thin, sallow, and quick-moving, with long brown hair tied back in a ponytail; and Ben Willard, the bassist, who was stocky and brown-skinned, his hair a torrent of narrow braids. It didn't take long for Asenath to glimpse each of their minds and know that she and her father would be safe riding with them; it didn't take much longer for her to catch the relationships among them. Kate and Vern were a couple, and Molly, Howie, and Ben were whatever you called a couple with three people in it—that wasn't something you saw among Innsmouth folk or most Starry Wisdom communities, but Asenath had heard of it among outsiders. She filed the knowledge away with an inward shrug.

She made the little unobtrusive motion the Esoteric Order of Dagon used to signal that all was well, and within a few minutes her father was making plans with Molly and Ben for the trip. Shortly thereafter she got a tour of the bus. The cab in front had two big bucket seats covered in fake green leather; behind, through a door, was something like a parlor, with a bench like a sofa on one side and chairs on swivels on the other. Further back was a kitchenette and a table with bench seats; behind that were bunk beds three deep, two sets of them on each side, with heavy sliding curtains to shut them off from the corridor; behind that, finally, was the bathroom. After that, Asenath and her father went back to the Shray's house for lunch and the time they had left with their friends. That went by in a flurry of talk and laughter. Only afterwards did Asenath recall that Robin had been unusually silent and pensive the whole time.

CHAPTER 4

THE CARDINAL WOODS

E ast out of Buffalo, Interstate 90 was still passable as far as Syracuse, maybe further, and I-81 north of there still had traffic on it. That was what Kate reported when she climbed aboard the bus the next morning. Asenath sat on the fake leather of the long bench seat and tried to imagine the trip ahead. A quarter hour earlier she'd said her goodbyes, scooped up her luggage and a big sack of groceries from the Buffalo public market, and followed her father and Cassie to the tour bus behind the warehouse.

"Then we're good," said Molly. "Everyone set? Okay."

Up in the cab, Vern did something Asenath couldn't see, and the engine whined its complaint and then lurched reluctantly to life. Cassie sent a panicked look down at the floor, then glanced at Asenath and, seeing her untroubled, closed her eyes and visibly composed herself. She jumped again when the bus started rolling, but calmed as the first rough movement settled into relative smoothness and the buildings began sliding decorously away.

The members of the band moved promptly into what Asenath guessed was their normal road routine. Kate trotted up to the cab and sat in the seat beside Vern's, watching the scenery ahead. Howie perched at the table beside the little kitchenette and buried himself in an old paperback book. Ben went to one of the beds in back, climbed in, pulled the curtain shut, and not long thereafter his snores blended melodiously with the low steady growl of the engine. That left Molly sprawled comfortably in a pivoting chair in what Asenath gathered was called the lounge, just back of the cab, and Owen, Asenath, and Cassie sat on the bench seat facing her, Cassie in her usual silence and the other two not quite sure what to say.

They didn't have to worry about that for long. "So I think you mentioned you live in Massachusetts." Molly said.

"Two of us do," said Asenath. "Cassie's local."

"Gotcha. Whereabouts in Massachusetts?"

"Arkham. It's up on the north coast past Salem."

"No kidding. J.J.'s on Fish Street used to be a good place. Any chance it's still there?"

Asenath was still trying to fit her mind around the fact that the famous Molly Wolejko knew about Arkham's sole music venue when her father said, "It's on Church Street now. We had some bad flooding two years ago, and there isn't much north of the river any more."

"I bet. That was the university neighborhood, wasn't it?" When he nodded: "Yeah, we played at J.J.'s a few times back in the day, when we were just a bunch of college kids with a sound that wasn't even that new yet. The audience ate it up, though."

She turned and looked out the window, where a half-empty commercial district was slipping past. "This is a real long shot," she said then, "but I knew somebody who moved up to Arkham years back, and I think I read something later about her still being there. Any chance you've heard of a woman about my age, plays the flute, used to go by Brecken Kendall?"

Once again, Owen spoke while Asenath was still blinking in amazement. "I hope so. Brecken teaches music at the school where I work, and she's also the organist at my church. A very sweet person."

"That's got to be the same one. Sweet was the right word when I knew her." Then, with a wry look: "I hope teaching music isn't all she does these days."

"Nope," said Asenath. "She writes operas."

"Seriously?" When Asenath nodded enthusiastically: "That's great. I actually got to hear the first thing she ever composed." Asenath gave her an astonished look, and Molly went on. "This was when we were both in college, and taking the same music class. Most of the kids were doing your standard avant-garde stuff, as dreadful as you'd expect, and there's this shy girl with her hair always falling into her face, and she goes up to the piano and plays this perfect Baroque bourrée in B flat."

"I know the piece," said Owen. "She plays a lot of her own stuff before and after church services, and plenty of people come early and stay late just to listen."

"I bet. So tell me about her operas."

Asenath and Owen between them described the three chamber operas they'd seen, and Molly nodded. "I want to hear the music from those someday."

Owen gave his daughter a speculative look. "You did quite a good job of Cassilda's song from *The King in Yellow* at the school talent show this spring, Sennie."

"Dad!" Asenath snapped, embarrassed.

"Give it a try," Molly said, grinning. "You already know what I sing like."

Asenath turned as red as her complexion permitted, glanced from one to the other, and realized that neither of them were joking. "Okay," she said, closed her eyes, and sang:

```
Along the shore the cloud waves break,
The two suns sink beneath the lake,
The shadows lengthen
             In Carcosa.
```

```
Strange is the night where black stars rise,
And strange moons circle through the skies,
But stranger still is
              Lost Carcosa.

Songs that the Hyades shall sing,
Where flap the tatters of the King,
Must die unheard in
              Dim Carcosa.

Song of my soul, my song is dead,
Die thou unsung, as tears unshed
Shall dry and die in
              Lost Carcosa.
```

She let the last note fade out into the muted grumbling of the engine and the slow rhythm of Ben's snoring, then opened her eyes. Her father was still smiling, just as she'd feared, but Molly was nodding with a slight frown on her face.

A moment later Howie said, "Okay, that's wild."

Asenath looked back toward him, not sure how to interpret it, but he went on: "Guess who I'm reading—Robert W. Chambers."

"Okay," said Owen, grinning. "You're right, that's wild. Which book?"

"It's an omnibus—*The King in Yellow*, *The Maker of Moons* and *The Mystery of Choice*."

"An omnibus on an omnibus," Molly said. Owen and Howie both laughed, and Asenath wondered why. An instant later she remembered where she'd heard of a Maker of Moons, and knew she needed to read the story. "So who's Robert W. Chambers?" she asked.

"A guy who wrote weird fiction," said Howie. "Like Lovecraft—you know who he was, right? Chambers put the song you just sang in one of his stories." Asenath made interested noises, and soon Howie had promised to lend her the book once he'd finished it.

A brief silence followed, or as close to silence as the engine's labors and Ben's snores permitted, and then Cassie turned to Owen and said, "Why did you say that was my song?"

Owen considered her. "Is Cassilda your full name?" She nodded. "Cassilda what?"

"I—I don't know," she said, visibly flustered. "Just Cassilda."

She did know. Asenath was sure of that. Someone had told her not to reveal her family name. Why? She filed the question with her other uncertainties about Cassie.

Owen explained to the girl about the character in the play *The King in Yellow*, and wondered aloud if Cassie had been named after her, but that got no response but a frightened look. Thereafter, though, Asenath noticed now and then that Cassie was watching Owen with an odd expression in her eyes, something halfway between fear and hope.

* * *

Howie was a fast reader, faster than anyone Asenath knew aside from her brother, and early the next afternoon she was curled up on the bench seat with the book in her hands, while the bus rolled onward, her father and Molly worked on lunch, and Cassie sat in silence with her hands in her lap and stared out the window, watching trees and farms and the very occasional truck go by. Syracuse was close by, but the farmers they'd met on the road warned them away from it—the city police had a reputation for seizing motor vehicles that were still in working order—so Vern had turned north on a county road and headed for the highway to Waterville. Lacking any better place to practice witchcraft, Asenath had gone into the bathroom and worked spells of protection, guidance, and concealment from there. How necessary those might be she had no idea, but she put as much voor into them as she could.

The stories by Robert W. Chambers made a helpful distraction from her worries, but the one she most wanted to read—"The Maker of Moons" itself—added puzzles of its own, not least because most of it was set in the Cardinal Woods. Once she'd finished it, she sat pondering it for a long while, sorting it out as though she meant to write a book report at school. Okay, she thought, the characters: Roy Cardenhe, the protagonist, whose last name sounded fake to her. His friends Pierpont the young idiot and Barris the government agent, and their servants—they were rich, Asenath gathered, like her best friend Emily's family. Ysonde, the love interest, who popped up out of nowhere. Her stepfather, a Chinese alchemist named Yue-Laou, who was the Maker of Moons and the Dzil-Nbu of the Kuen-Yuin, whatever that meant. Some government agents, some dogs, and some creatures that looked like crabs or spiders.

She had finished making the mental list when three things occurred to her. The first was that Cassie, like Ysonde, had popped up out of nowhere; the second was that Ysonde didn't have a family name either, and the third was that like Cassie, Ysonde lived in a little house in the Cardinal Woods with her stepfather, but before then had lived in Yian. The story and the circumstances of Cassie's appearance had far too much in common for accident to explain it—but what did that mean? Asenath stared blankly at the pages, trying to assemble the scraps of knowledge she had into something that made sense, and got nowhere.

Back in the little kitchenette, her father and Mollie were making sandwiches and talking about Brecken Kendall. "That's good to hear," said Molly. "I hope the bus lasts long enough to get us to Arkham. I'd like to have the chance to see her again and hear some of her music."

Owen said something agreeable, but Asenath turned to the next story in the book and tried not to show her disquiet. She'd already figured out that Molly Wolejko knew a fair amount about the Great Old Ones and the elder races, but only as things in stories by H.P. Lovecraft, not as things you could meet in the waking world. Plenty of wry stories and edged jokes among the people of the Great Old Ones recounted what happened when outsiders suddenly discovered that the world was bigger and stranger than they had been taught. For that matter, Asenath had heard her father's stories of his own struggle to deal with that discovery the autumn that he'd found his way to Innsmouth and then to Dunwich, and nearly died in the process.

Suppose Molly Wolejko and the other members of the band make it to Arkham, Asenath thought. Suppose they pay a visit to Ms. Kendall in her house on Pickman Street, and suppose they find out that Ms. Kendall has a partner, and the partner is a shoggoth. Marriages between different species were common enough among the people of the Great Old Ones that nobody gave that a second thought. When Asenath had first heard about it, in an excited letter from Emily Chaudronnier one bright spring day in Dunwich, she'd simply filed it as one of the things grown-ups did, far less important than her upcoming move to Arkham and the three orphaned kyrrmi pups she was raising just then. Shoggoths were already part of Asenath's world—a colony of them lived under Sentinel Hill near Dunwich, and her parents had a shoggoth living in their basement for a while, a small one who'd escaped from a different colony the Radiance had destroyed—and once she settled in Arkham and was introduced to Ms. Kendall's partner Sho, the pleasant conversation that followed settled any remaining uncertainties she might have had.

Could Molly Wolejko see things that way, though? Could she sit down to talk with a creature that looked a little like a mound of iridescent black soap bubbles dotted with pale green eyes, and see the person there, shy, gentle, crazy in love with Ms. Kendall and just as devoted to the six shoggoth broodlings they were raising together? For that matter, what would Molly think about the people in Arkham who had tentacles in place of legs or arms or both, or Robin, or the Deep Ones who came up the Miskatonic River to visit their relatives in town? Could she cope with those, too? Or would she shriek in terror and run away as fast as she could, and maybe do something that would bring a Radiance negation team down on them all?

In the kitchenette, the sandwich-making continued, though Asenath's father and Molly were talking about roads now, where it was safe to cross the Hudson on the way to Massachusetts, how to get to the Aylesbury Pike from there. "You want to be careful when you're leaving Aylesbury, though," said Owen. "There's a little road going left off the Pike about a mile out of town, and if you take it you're on the road to Dunwich. The road's still fine last I heard, but it'll add at least an hour to your driving time."

"Dunwich?" Howie said, glancing up from another book. "As in 'The Dunwich Horror?' Any Whateleys living up that way these days?"

"Quite a few of them," Owen said, not missing a beat. "But Wilbur and his brother haven't been seen since 1928, you know." Howie laughed and returned to his book.

A glance at Cassie showed her still staring out the window, but she had a fixed, tense expression on her face that Asenath hadn't seen there before. A moment passed, and Asenath shrugged inwardly and started reading the next story in the book.

* * *

The tour bus reached Cardinal Springs early on the third day of the trip. Not long after dawn that day, Asenath scrambled out of the bunk bed where she'd slept the night, washed and dressed in the bathroom, and followed the scent of cooking breakfast forward to the lounge. The windows on either side showed thick forest, dotted here and there with little roadside buildings that had been abandoned for years. Her father had been up for a while already, she guessed, and he and Howie were in the middle of a lively conversation about H.P. Lovecraft. Kate and Ben were cooking breakfast, Vern was driving as always, and Molly and Cassie were still asleep. Asenath greeted everyone and plopped down on the bench seat.

An hour later, the forest had begun to give way to outlying farms, and Asenath went to get her suitcase packed and then helped Cassie pack hers. When the two of them came back into the lounge with their luggage, Cardinal Springs spread out in front of them, a farm town noticeably less dilapidated than those Asenath knew. A scattering of cars and trucks still sat parked on the streets but makeshift hitching posts for horses had sprung up in front of bars and shops. Toward the center of town they spotted a motel with a garish sign that said VACANCY; Owen spoke to Molly, Molly went forward to speak to Vern, and the tour bus glided gracefully to a halt by the sidewalk outside the motel's front door.

Hands got shaken then, the front door hissed and clanked open, and Owen, Asenath, and Cassie went down the stair with their luggage while the members of the band wished them well. The door closed, and then the bus engine gave out a grinding noise and shuddered to a halt. Asenath gave her father a worried look. He waited on the sidewalk, and after a moment Vern came out with a toolbox and busied himself with the engine. Molly came down the steps a moment later. Owen said, "What's the plan if it won't start?"

That got him a grin. "Either we settle down here in Cardinal Springs or we see if the schooner you talked about has room for five musicians and their instruments." In response to Owen's questioning look: "Oh, it'll be probably be the schooner, but we'll have to vote. That's what we agreed when we left Seattle better than two years ago."

Just as Asenath was starting to think about sailing back to Arkham with a metal band, Vern finished with the engine, slammed down the panel, and went back into the cab. A moment later the engine growled sullenly to life. Molly grinned again and climbed back up the stair; the door wheezed shut, gears clattered and complained, and the tour bus rolled on. Asenath watched it go and wondered if she'd ever see any of the band members again. Owen motioned to the two girls with the hand that wasn't holding a suitcase, and led the way into the motel.

Asenath was used to motels, but only the kind owned by the people of the Great Old Ones, which always went out of their way to chase off outsiders. This one lacked the familiar trappings—the pictures of local landscapes made to look dreary and dangerous, the paint and fabric colors that swore acidly at one another, and the rest of it—but it managed the same effect by a sort of weary blandness. The middle-aged woman behind the front desk greeted them formulaically, asked some desultory questions, brightened when Owen gave her a few small glittering shapes in place of a wad of bills sure to lose half their value over the next year or so.

A few minutes later Asenath followed her father and Cassie to their rooms, which were on the second floor, with windows looking south across a parking lot and a scattering of old houses. Owen had rented two rooms with a door connecting them, one for himself and one for them. "I want the two of you to stay here for now," he said once they were inside the girls' room with the door shut. "Once I've had the chance to look around and figure out how safe we are here, we can make other plans. Expect me back before lunchtime."

Asenath nodded and then motioned for him to wait, and her father laughed and bowed slightly. With three fingers of her right hand, she traced a complicated geometrical pattern over his forehead and then said in a low voice, "As Haon-Dor passed unnoticed among his enemies, so pass thou unnoticed among thine." Voor flowed and shimmered as the spell came together. Owen grinned, thanked her, wished them both a pleasant couple of hours, and left the room.

She turned to find Cassie staring at her. "What was that?"

Flustered—she'd unthinkingly shown sorcery to an outsider—Asenath managed nonetheless to keep her face from showing it. "Oh, it's just a blessing. It's part of our religion."

"Oh," said Cassie. She was silent for a long moment, then asked in a tentative voice, "Do you know about a place called Dunwich?"

Asenath had looked out the window to hide her embarrassment, but turned back, startled. "What do you know about Dunwich?"

Cassie swallowed visibly, and then said, "Howie mentioned it, and my stepfather used to talk about it. It's got stones on the hills, like the ones on the place where—where I met you."

Asenath took that in. "Yes, it does," she said after another moment. "I was born in Dunwich, and lived there until I was eight."

"What—what's it like there?"

Memories came surging up. "It's a little town, not much more than one street, with a school and a church and a library and a general store, and mountains and woods all around it. It's really pretty." A smile forced its way out. "Arkham, where I live now, is really nice too, but sometimes I miss the mountains, and I know a lot of people there."

"Oh," said Cassie. A silence followed, and then Cassie went to the window. Asenath followed. Off in the distance, beyond the houses, pines rose dark.

"The Cardinal Woods?" Asenath asked her.

"I think so," said Cassie. "It looks just like the woods around my stepfather's house."

"Well, good. With any luck we'll find him for you."

Cassie nodded, said nothing.

* * *

Owen was back before lunchtime as he'd promised, and flopped in an armchair while the two girls perched on one of the beds. "So far, so good," he said. "The town still gets enough traffic that strangers don't stick out like sore thumbs. I talked to two waitresses, a librarian, and a guy who runs a martial arts school, and I think I know where to find your stepfather."

Cassie's face lit up, and she thanked him repeatedly. When she'd finished, Asenath gave him a skeptical look. "There's a martial arts school here?"

Owen laughed. "I thought the same thing. Yeah, he has a storefront here and he teaches classes in two other towns—Fernville's one of them." After a blank moment, Asenath recalled that as the name of the town where they would meet the *Abigail Prinn* in a few days. "He's an interesting guy. He teaches a traditional kung-fu style, one I've never heard of. You can ask him about it if you want to; I've arranged for the three of us to have lunch with him in an hour."

"Mr. Merrill," Cassie said, "is it okay if I stay here instead?" Owen gave her a questioning look, and she huddled into herself. "I've spent so much time around people I don't know, and they've all been really nice to me, but I'm not used to that."

"That won't be any kind of problem," Owen replied. "There's a sub sandwich shop across the street; we can get some takeout for you there before we go."

That got settled readily enough. Asenath and her father went to the sandwich place, Asenath took a sandwich and a glass of lemonade back to the hotel room, and then she rejoined her father and walked alongside him down the sidewalks of Cardinal Springs. It looked like a pleasant town, she thought, not that different from Arkham in many ways, full of storefronts that had been built for local shops, housed national chains for a while, and had reverted to local shops again. The diner where Owen stopped and pulled open the door for her was no exception. By the look of it, some hamburger franchise had been there for a while, but the big illuminated plastic sign had been taken down—she could see the marks where it had been—and a smaller, painted wooden sign put in its place, bearing just one word: ANNIE'S.

That was promising, and the smells that greeted Asenath as she went in were more promising still, but most of her attention was on the man seated at the table nearest the door, who smiled and stood up as she and her father came in. Tall and muscular, he had dark brown skin and a shaved head, and moved with the fluid grace she'd seen in other martial artists. Those weren't the focus of her attention, though.

Voor flowed through him like a river. That was what she noticed first about him. She'd sensed something like that in a few elderly masters of *khrang tayeng*, once in an aikido teacher who'd come up from Providence on Starry Wisdom Church business and taught a few classes while she was there, and also in some of the witches and sorceresses she knew. To find a martial arts teacher with that mastery of power in a little farm town, she thought, was a little like meeting one of the Great Old Ones—

In a music venue in Buffalo? She thought of Nyarlathotep, and wondered if she'd strayed into much deeper waters than she'd expected.

By then her father was making introductions. "Asenath, this is Sifu Dennis Cooper. Dennis, my daughter Asenath. Cassie wasn't feeling well, so she's resting at the hotel." Hands got shaken—his were as massive and strong as the rest of him—and they sat down. The next few minutes went into consulting the menu, which was handwritten on a white plastic board on one wall, and ordering lunch, and after that a few more minutes went into ordinary pleasantries. After that, though, Cooper turned to Asenath and said, "From the way you move, I'm going to guess you've had some martial arts training yourself."

"Well, a little," Asenath admitted. It wasn't always safe to mention the Tcho-Tchos around outsiders, but she had a usefully vague response to hand. "I've got friends whose families came here as refugees after the Vietnam War, and I learned from one of their aunts." Memories hovered around those words: an elderly aunt of Evan's who taught a dozen girls after school in the back yard of the Shray house, passing on movements that, by tradition, no man was ever allowed to see except in actual combat. "It was mostly self-defense."

"That's good to hear," said Cooper, turning slightly to include Owen in the conversation. "I'd like to see a lot more girls get martial arts training, so they can protect themselves, but also to give them the kind of confidence you get from knowing you can hold your own in a fight."

Owen nodded, and Asenath said, "Dad said you teach a style he's never heard of."

"That doesn't surprise me too much," Cooper said. "Not a lot of people know about—" Here he said three words in what Asenath guessed was Chinese; they sounded like *chwan yuan chwan.* "It's an old southern Chinese style from up in the mountains, but I learned it in Brooklyn, where I grew up. I used to catch the bus down to this little storefront school off 8th Avenue in Sunset Park four, five times a week after school. Mom thought it was great because it kept me out of trouble." The waitress came out with their lunches and made a little small talk, and once she was gone, Cooper said, "So remind me about the girl and her—stepfather, was it?"

Owen nodded, and explained about Cassie while Asenath got to work on her club sandwich. "Okay," Cooper said when he was finished. "I'm pretty sure I know where you have to go, then. Cardinal Woods State Park's just south of here—you go up D Street and you'll get to the Sweet Fern Trail, which leads right into the middle of it past Lake of the Stars—but like a lot of the parks here, it's got a few chunks of private property in it. If you go up the trail I just mentioned, you're right alongside one of those, and there are some houses up that way. If she was living with her stepfather in the Cardinal Woods, that's got to be where it was." He considered Owen for a moment. "Has she said much about her stepfather?"

"Next to nothing," Owen replied. Then: "She hasn't told us everything she knows. I've been sure of that since about an hour after I first met her."

Cooper nodded. "I bet. Kids are like that sometimes."

If you only knew, Asenath thought.

* * *

She left the motel that afternoon with her father and Cassie, walked together up cracked and broken sidewalks and then on potholed streets once the sidewalks ran out. As Cooper had promised, D Street ran straight up to the edge of the forest and stopped at a trailhead and a big parking lot that hadn't had a car on it for many months, to judge from the weeds poking up through the sparse gravel. Where the parking lot gave way to the trail's mouth, a wooden sign rose up, with words in faded yellow paint:

CARDINAL WOODS STATE PARK
Sweet Fern Trail
Lake of the Stars 11 Miles

Before they started up the trail, Owen turned to Cassie. "If anything we pass looks familiar, let me know." She looked up at him and ventured a smile.

The trail was easy going, a broad dirt path well tamped down by generations of hikers' boots, winding in long leisurely curves into the distance beneath soaring white pines and sugar maples. Cardinals flew here and there, bright spots of red, and once as they neared a stream, a great blue heron went by overhead with great slow flaps of its wings. Asenath kept half her attention on the forest around her and half of it on Cassie, and noted the sudden widening of the girl's eyes a moment before she spoke.

"Yes," she said. "I've—I've been this way before."

Owen nodded. "On this trail?"

"I think so."

Time passed and so did the landscape. They came to a big gray boulder jutting up from the soil, half mantled in moss and surrounded by pines, and Cassie broke into a broad smile. "Yes," she said again. "I used to play here." She went over to the boulder, and Asenath followed.

"There was a trail," Cassie said then. "Near here—"

A thin trail, no more than a deer track, veered off from the main path. "This way," Cassie said, her voice more confident. They followed her, and after a little while passed a maple with an weathered and rusted sign saying PRIVATE PROPERTY. Cassie ignored it and went on, her pace picking up. "Yes," she said then. "Yes! It's just a little farther."

The trail led up a low rise mantled in pines, and then down again into denser woods. Dim gray shapes loomed amid the trees, and Asenath's blood ran cold for a moment, for they looked like hooded figures standing there, shoulders hunched, heads bowed. Another few steps down the trail and she could see them more clearly: stones, a rough circle of them amid the trees, each stone a little taller than her father. Off in the further distance she caught a glimpse of something else gray, but the trees were too thick for her to see what it was.

"Sennie," Cassie said then in a low voice. "Thank you. You've been really nice to me." Then she broke into a run, toward the stone circle. Owen called her name, warning, but she ignored him and kept running. After a startled moment, Asenath went after her, but by then Cassie was well ahead, and put on a burst of speed as she heard footfalls. She passed the nearest of the stones while Asenath was still half a dozen yards behind her. For an instant the stone hid her; then she cried out "Stepfather!" in what sounded like relief—

And Asenath broke through into the stone circle to find no one there.

She stopped, looked this way, that. Cassie had vanished. She called a spell to mind, one that would find things that had been lost, and cast it, twisting her fingers together in the requisite pattern and murmuring the words under her breath. Nothing happened.

In another moment her father was beside her. "Gone?"

She looked up at him. "I can't find her even with a spell."

"Do you think it was—" He left the rest unsaid. Even in the solitude of the Cardinal Woods, there were things it was not safe to mention aloud.

She blinked, and wanted to kick herself for not thinking of the gift she'd received from Phauz, the power no one else on the lesser Earth had—or was that true? There was only one way to find out. Without Rachel it was harder, but she closed her eyes, folded her hands together, and let her inner vision turn toward a continuum that wasn't space or time as humans knew them, a realm of vast prismatic shapes of no earthly colors, of angles that made no sense at all, of a constant shrieking and roaring confusion of sound. Movement through that realm left tracks that lingered, and she'd learned to sense those, but the not-substance around her was still.

She blinked again. "It wasn't that," she said. "What are we going to do?"

"Search the area." He looked around. "She appeared in a stone circle, didn't she? My guess is that she's back with her stepfather. But we should make sure."

Asenath nodded uneasily, started around the stone circle, first inside it and then outside. She was most of the way around the second time when she saw or thought she saw something scurrying away on the ground: a quick blur of movement, a sense of many legs and of something yellow. It was gone before she could be sure she'd actually seen anything, and when she went to where she thought it had been, she found nothing. She shrugged, kept searching.

An hour or so later, standing on the trail outside the stone circle, they glanced at each other, and Owen said. "I think we've found what there is to find." They'd been all over that corner of the woods, and other than the crablike thing Asenath thought she'd seen, spotted only two things. One was a long-abandoned cottage of stone with a half-collapsed wooden roof, the gray shape Asenath had glimpsed past the stone circle. If anyone had lived there in the last half century, they'd left no trace behind.

The second thing was in Owen's hand as they stood there: a stone Chinese seal of what looked like pale green jade, some two inches long and three quarters of an inch square, with the head of some unknown beast carved on one end and a flat surface engraved with strange characters on the other. He'd found it, buried deep under debris, in a corner of the abandoned cottage. Asenath had sensed nothing there, though she'd searched the cottage more than once, but some initiate's power had led her father straight to it.

"Any idea why it was there?" she asked him.

"Maybe Yue-Laou left it," Owen said. When she gave him a puzzled look: "The character from 'The Maker of Moons.' Remember? He lived in the Cardinal Woods."

Asenath tried to figure out whether he was joking, gave up after a moment. He pocketed the seal, motioned toward the trail back to Cardinal Springs. She gave him an unhappy look but nodded, and started walking that way when he did.

CHAPTER 5

THE VOICES OF THE SEA

"Don't worry about it," said Dennis Cooper. The engine of his car made alarming noises but started anyway, and he gunned it, shifted into gear. "I've got a class to teach in Fernville at seven, and I want to get some shopping done first—you see stuff in the shops down in Fernville we never get up here." The car lurched into motion and rolled out of the parking lot.

Owen said something or other polite. Sitting in the back seat of Cooper's Ford, next to the luggage, Asenath looked out the window at the buildings of Cardinal Springs and the forest beyond it, thinking about Cassie: her sudden appearance and disappearance, the mysteries that surrounded her. The last words she'd said before vanishing sounded too much like a farewell for Asenath's comfort, the sort of thing you said to someone you didn't expect to see again.

In front, her father and Cooper talked easily about the local economy, what the farmers in Adams County were growing, what they might be interested in selling and buying. Except for the fine details, it was a conversation Asenath had heard many times before over the years just past. She'd studied it in school, too: the fading out of the age of mass production and mass marketing, the return of local and regional trade networks, and the rest. It was important, she knew that, but just then she had to struggle to keep that in mind.

The road to Fernville unrolled ahead, a winding gray line bordered with forest and the occasional farm. Overhead, the day turned toward afternoon. She'd slept poorly the night before, brooding over Cassie, and before long the steady drone of the engine and the rocking of the car had its effect and she leaned back and dozed off.

She didn't expect to find her way into the Dreamlands, not without Rachel's help and not dozing in the back of someone else's car, but before long she found herself on a stone stair lit from below by flames. She knew where she was at once, and finished the journey down the seventy steps to the cavern of flame where the priests Nasht and Kaman-Tha make offerings to the gods of dream. The two priests turned to regard her as she entered, their onyx eyes featureless, their long narrow beards bound up in the Egyptian style; she curtseyed to them, waited for any questions they might ask, but they simply nodded, approving her descent, and returned to their endless rites. She curtseyed again, beaming, and trotted down the seven hundred steps to the Gates of Deeper Slumber and the Enchanted Wood beyond.

That was familiar territory. She made a fluttering call to alert the creatures that dwell in the wood that she meant no harm and sought no favors, and then spent a few moments searching for three perfect mushrooms, which she put in her shoulderbag. That done, she headed north beneath tall trees toward the river Oukranos and the jasper terraces of Kiran. Though pale eyes regarded her from the shadows of the trees, she passed unchallenged through the wood and came to the river as the sun of the Dreamlands sank past the shoulder of Mount Thurai to the west.

The great bridge of Kiran, carved from a single mass of pale yellow jasper, arched over the river there to the seven-pinnacled temple on the far bank, but Asenath turned aside from the path, walked down to the riverbank, and sat there. After a little while, she whistled a polite greeting in the language of shoggoths, which was made of musical notes. There were no shoggoths in Kiran, or if there were she had never met one, but the fish who swim in the waters of the Oukranos rise and show themselves in response to a whistled tune, and it was a private joke of Asenath's to whistle shoggoth-words to them.

The fish never seemed to mind. Within a few minutes three of them, sprightly and iridescent, darted just beneath the surface of the water as though dancing for her. That cheered her, and she was distracted enough by their antics that she didn't notice another shape, round and pale, rising slowly up from the depths of the river, until it was nearly at the surface.

Startled, she nonetheless remembered the proper words of greeting when the river-wight's head broke through the water. Pale-skinned, with hair green and flat as seaweed, it grinned at her with its long sharp teeth and said, "What will you give me if I tell you the thing you most wish to know?"

Asenath pulled the mushrooms out of her shoulderbag and held them out on her palm—she had picked them with precisely this chance in mind, having long since learned the ways of river-wights. The creature's eyes widened and it said, "Yes, yes! Give them to me!"

"Bind yourself first to tell me the truth," said Asenath. Once the river-wight had uttered the words of binding, she tossed the mushrooms to it one at a time, and it lunged for them, snapping them out of the air. Once it had swallowed the last, it closed its eyes for a little while in evident pleasure, then said, "You will see her again. Watch for her after the leaves fall." Before Asenath could say anything in response, it plunged back down into the water and vanished from sight. She stared after it, mouth open, amazed.

Then she was blinking awake in the back seat of Cooper's car, and her father was standing at the open door, saying, "Wake up, sleepyhead. We're here."

She blinked, rubbed her eyes, found enough clarity to help haul the luggage out from the back seat and to realize that the car was stopped in front of another motel. Once the luggage was out, she and Owen thanked Cooper, who grinned, wished them a safe trip home, and drove off.

* * *

They had to wait two days in Fernville before the *Abigail Prinn* arrived. It might have been a dull time or a fretful one—Fernville was smaller than Cardinal Springs, and owed its existence solely to the river traffic and an earnest little ferry that crossed to a similarly sized village on the Canadian side—but Asenath had tucked her copy of *The Book of Eibon* into an inner pocket of her suitcase, hoping to study it once Cassie was back with her stepfather. Now that Cassie was gone, out it came, and she had the advantage of a father who was a schoolteacher and a sixth-degree initiate in the Starry Wisdom Church to help her find a way through the intricacies of that ancient and notoriously opaque tome.

They quickly fell into a rhythm, discussing this or that passage until Asenath's brain felt full to bursting, going for walks along the riverside where a park waited in vain for the tourists of an earlier day, eating a meal in one of Fernville's two restaurants, and then returning to the book for another round of eldritch lore. Even so, she was glad when a stray glance upriver finally showed the white sails of the schooner making its earnest way toward the quay. Settling the bill with the motel clerk took only a few minutes, and she and Owen were standing a few paces back from the quayside, luggage in hand, as the sails came down, the *Abigail Prinn* slid up against the quay, and the sailors sprang ashore with heavy ropes in hand.

The purser was already on deck, and waved. Owen waved back and crossed the quay with Asenath at his heels. One long step from quay to gangway and she was aboard; Owen and the purser exchanged a few words, and then the purser called out to the first mate, who shouted orders to the sailors. By the time the sailors loosed the ship, Asenath was already following her father down the well-worn ladder to the deck below.

She made a beeline for her cabin amidships, and ducked into the cramped little space. Her suitcase went on the floor for the time being and she perched on the bed, the routine familiar to her, the need to keep out of the way of the sailors and officers another familiarity. The schooner was moving again, finding its balance between the wind and the river current; footfalls, many of them, drummed on the deck above her head; through the half-open door she could hear her father's voice, Larry Shray's, and then another voice, more distant, the first mate shouting orders again. The deck shifted again beneath her feet. A glance out the porthole showed the schooner and the far riverbank running more or less in parallel. She scrambled off the berth and got her things packed away in the drawers beneath it, tucked the *Book of Eibon* in a place where she could get it easily, and had gotten to her feet again just as the purser stuck his head in to tell her she could leave her cabin if she liked.

He went on to the next door, and before she could decide what she wanted to do next, Evan Shray stood in the doorway, his plain round face tense in a way she didn't recognize. Once they got ordinary greetings out of the way, he asked, "So what happened with Cassie? Did you find her stepfather?"

"Dad and I think so," Asenath said.

That got her a disbelieving look. "You *think* so?"

Asenath motioned for him to come in and close the door; not all the sailors aboard the *Abigail Prinn* were from Arkham, and she didn't want to talk too freely around outsiders. Once the door clicked shut, she said, "Do you remember what I said about the way she just appeared out of nowhere in the stone circle on Elk Hill? She led us to a stone circle in the woods, then ran to it and called to her stepfather and—" A gesture mimed her disappearance. "Gone."

"You didn't look for her?"

"Of course we looked for her," said Asenath, wondering why he sounded so upset. "We spent an hour searching all around there, and I used some spells I know."

"But you don't know what happened to her," he said. "You don't know at all." He turned sharply, pulled the door open. Over his shoulder, in angry tones: "I'd have kept looking." He slammed the door behind him, and a moment later she heard another door slam open and shut.

Baffled, she went to her door, opened it and leaned out. The companionway was empty all the way aft to the ladder except for Robin, who'd opened his door and leaned out a moment before she had and was looking away from her. He turned at the sound of her movements, saw her, gave her a dismayed look, and vanished back into his cabin. Asenath tried to make sense of that, gave up, and went back into her cabin.

She had better things to do than worry about boys, or so she told herself. Once the door was latched and the flimsy cloth curtain pulled across the cabin's one porthole, she got a piece of chalk out of her shoulderbag and drew a curious diagram of angled lines on the inside of the door, the one convenient flat surface the cabin had. A few words in a language older than vertebrate life on Earth, and the lines flared with purple light—

And she plunged into a shrieking, roaring abyss where strange prismatic shapes loomed up around her and grotesque presences twisted and writhed. It took her a little while to find the familiar route, but before long she was hurtling forward through immensities, toward a place where two masses folded together at an angle not quite so incomprehensible as the rest. Another instant and she was stepping out of an unlit corner in a cramped little room she knew well: the spare bedroom in Betty Hale's house.

A brown ratlike shape curled up on the pillow looked up, startled, then let out a shrill little cry and bounded over toward her. "Yes, I missed you too," Asenath said, scooping Rachel up from the foot of the bed. "I hope you behaved yourself. Now let's go find Betty and thank her, and we can go."

The house was empty, though, and certain items missing from their places told Asenath that the witch had gone to help at a birth; Penny Moore's baby must have come early, she guessed. It took a little searching to find a pen that worked and some paper, but a few moments later she'd written a note thanking Betty Hale for taking care of Rachel, and went back to the spare bedroom. The spell reopened the portal, and Asenath flung herself back through the shrieking abyss, paced this time by a shifting polyhedron of many colors she knew as Rachel.

They were back inside the cabin after what seemed like minutes and was actually a fraction of a second—she'd timed it once, out of curiosity. A handkerchief from her shoulderbag erased all trace of the chalk drawing on the back of the door, and then she lay back on the bed, feeling tired. Rachel climbed up onto her chest and chirred at her, and she said, "I'll be okay. It's just been kind of a long week." Then, in response to another chirr: "Yes, I'll remember everything I did so you can see it. I wish you could do that for me."

Unbidden, an image rose in her mind: Rachel curled up on the pillow in Betty Hale's spare room, sound asleep. Asenath laughed and said, "I bet."

* * *

A brisk wind out of the northwest filled the sails of the *Abigail Prinn* in the hours and days that followed, as the shores of the St. Lawrence slid past, dotted with towns in various stages of dilapidation and survival. Most of the time, when Asenath traveled to Chorazin for the summer and back, she watched the scenery avidly. Early on, when she'd made the trip in her father's big brown station wagon, the hills and woods and dilapidated farms of western Massachusetts and upstate New York had become a litany of images she could recount by heart. Once the roads got too bad, fuel became hard to find, and schooners started making the once-familiar voyage from New England to the Great Lakes and back by way of the St. Lawrence, that route took on the same role in Asenath's imagination, a memory to be recalled when chores became dull or a teacher had to explain to another pupil some point Asenath had already grasped.

This time, though, she paid little attention to the hills and fields and clustered roofs on both shores, not even when they passed Montréal and its mostly empty skyscrapers. Partly that was because Cassie's disappearance still haunted her, but her fellow passengers contributed their share as well. Evan stayed upset, with a brittle politeness he always settled into when he had to stifle anger. When the weather was good, he found a place on deck the sailors didn't need and practiced his *khrang tayeng* forms with furious intensity, driving himself until his punches and palm strikes were almost too fast for her eyes to follow and his kicks struck hard higher than his own head. When the weather was bad he stayed in his cabin most of the time and rarely spoke to anyone but his parents and his sisters. Asenath watched him, feeling baffled and upset.

That would have been difficult enough by itself. What made the voyage all but intolerable was Robin—or more precisely the near-absence of Robin. In years past, even after the easy cameraderie of their childhoods had fallen away, they'd spent much of the voyage talking about the events of the summer and the prospects for the school year about to begin, and when Newfoundland was in sight he'd always read aloud the old narrative his ancestor Jan Maertens had written about his voyage to the New World before the time of Columbus, a ritual of sorts that rounded off the summer.

This time, though, as the *Abigail Prinn* made her way down the St. Lawrence River to the sea, Robin avoided her, vanishing belowdecks whenever she came up the ladder and finding seats in the messroom at meals where she couldn't sit near him. The familiar sound of his dulcimer, which he'd played by the hour on past voyages, was as absent as he was, and the silence unnerved her more than she wanted to admit. When she confronted him about it on the second day of the voyage, his only response was to look away and say, "I don't want to talk about it," and since they were never alone on the crowded schooner she couldn't work up the courage to embarrass them both in public by pressing the issue. Lacking his company, she holed up in her cabin for long hours, trying to distract herself with the nested obscurities of the *Book of Eibon*, feeling angry at him, at herself, and at the world in general.

The wind held good as the schooner reached salt water and headed for Cabot Strait, fast enough that the bow wave foamed white—"with a bone in her teeth," the sailors said. In due time the low dark line of Newfoundland's shore rose up ahead to port. That day at lunch, miserable and out of patience, Asenath cornered Robin in the messroom and said, "I hope you'll at least read the story of Jan Maertens to me so this summer isn't a complete loss."

He glanced up at her, startled, and the expression on his face nearly made her burst into tears: she hadn't realized until that moment that he was just as miserable as she was, and she searched her memories thereafter to try to think of something she might have done to cause that. "I can do that," he said, looking away again. "See you on deck in a minute."

She didn't have to force a smile. "Sure thing."

It took more than a minute, but presently the two of them were on deck a little forward of the mainmast, both of them bundled up in warm coats—though the weather was better than Cabot Strait usually saw, and the bright sun of late summer streamed down through clear skies, the air felt cold and the occasional flurries of spray that whipped past were colder still. Asenath didn't care. She settled on a locker, tucked her hands into her pockets, and listened.

" 'I was twenty-six years of age,'" Robin read aloud from the old photocopy, "'when I took ship in the free city of Lübeck as a man-at-arms on the cog *Mary of Bremen*, on the feast of the apostles Philip and James, it being the eleventh day of May in the year of grace 1456...'" The familiar words traced out a tale Asenath knew by heart, the story of an ordinary Dutch man-at-arms who went west over seas to the New World a generation before Columbus for a terrible purpose he never understood. Long before the village of Chorazin rose beside Elk Hill, he had been there, survived what was done in Elk Hill's shadow, and made his way back to Europe at last with the help of Portuguese fishermen, bearing with him all unknowing a legacy that eventually brought Robin's father to Chorazin in turn. Jan Maertens had seen other things on his voyage, though, and one of them haunted Asenath's thoughts as the story came to an end.

"What are you thinking?" Robin asked then. He always asked her that and she always asked the same thing of him, part of the little ritual of the story. She had to struggle to keep from bursting into tears when he said it, but this time they were tears of relief.

"Greenland," she told him. "I keep on wondering why the other side killed everybody who lived there. It just doesn't make sense." With a little shrug: "And they always have reasons for what they do. Bad reasons, but reasons."

"Did you hear what Dr. Gilman said about that?"

"No," she admitted. "Which Dr. Gilman?"

Robin nodded, conceding the point. Toby and Leah Gilman were friends of their parents who came down from Maine every year or two, and both of them had doctorates. "Toby. He and my dad got talking about that one night and I sat there and listened. Dr. Gilman said that the other side killed everyone, and then they searched everywhere and dug holes in the ground. They were looking for something, but nobody knows what."

"I wonder what it was," said Asenath, and watched the dim line of Newfoundland slide past in the distance. Robin didn't answer, and she was grateful for that. For a moment, an echo of their old friendship seemed to hover in the air between them, and she worried that a misjudged word might disperse that. The voices of the sea spoke instead, harsh, wordless, reassuring.

* * *

After that, the rest of the voyage was a little less difficult for Asenath. Something still raised a barrier between her and Robin, but it was a barrier that could be crossed. Not long after the *Abigail Prinn* headed out of Cabot Strait and into the open Atlantic, a nor'easter blew in, and that simplified things a little as well; while the storm lasted, no one but the crew went on deck, and Asenath could hole up in her cabin and put hours into trying to make sense of the *Book of Eibon* without feeling as though she was hiding from anyone. The part of the book she was reading helped, since it recounted a series of improbable events on the planet that Asenath knew as Saturn and Eibon called Cykranosh, and those very quickly put her in the state of enticing bafflement that the more elusive passages in the old tomes always brought with them. Was the whole tale a parable, or was Saturn actually much more Earthlike in Eibon's day? The Djhibbis, those strange flightless Saturnian birds who spent their lives perched on rocks contemplating the mystic syllables *yop*, *yeep*, and *yoop*—were they part of the fauna of Cykranosh, or metaphors passsing on an arcane wisdom, or just a manifestation of Eibon's legendary dry humor?

Such puzzles kept her distracted as the schooner ran before the wind with Nova Scotia off her starboard rail and the open Atlantic to port. So did her dreams. With Rachel's help she slept ten hours or more each night, and spent the time in the Dreamlands, most of it walking west along the shores of the Cerenerian Sea. One night she had to contend with harpies, but escaped unharmed. Another brought her to a half-sunk temple of Mother Hydra on the seashore, where she stripped and waded through shoulder-deep water to the altar to pray in the familiar liquid syllables of the Deep Ones' language. Still another night she came to the beach where slept the worse than shapeless thing the old Greeks concealed under the legend of Proteus, but she knew better than to risk rousing it and slipped past unnoticed.

Finally she reached the city of Ogrothan a day's journey past the Straits of Stethelos, where the Twilight Sea flows into the Cerenerian Sea between high pale crags. All gray stone and age-silvered wood, Ogrothan gleamed before her as she came down the trail beneath the uncertain light of a foggy day, and sky-blue gulls wheeled overhead, calling to one another in their desolate voices. The seaward half of the city bustled, and big painted galleons from Hlanith and Celephaïs sat at anchor in the harbor, but further inland the streets were empty in daylight—they would be busy enough come nightfall, but no safe place for a mortal dreamer.

The temple of Tamash, her destination, loomed up into the mists at the landward end of the town, surrounded on three sides by cedars of immense size and antiquity. She knelt three times before entering the great ivory doors of the temple, which always stand with one half open and the other shut, and walked the length of the great hall within. At its end, before the silver statue of Tamash, smoke billowed perpetually from an iron hearth. Watched carefully, the smoke would sometimes reveal hidden things, but she stared at it for a long while without learning anything. Only in the instant before she turned to go did she catch three uncertain shapes above the hearth: a face that might have been Cassie's, a shore seen across open water that reminded her of Newfoundland, and a small black shape like a statue, though she could not tell its form. Through the dim faint images moved something else: a sense of distant shapes moving, of some vast architecture of events unknown to her that spread outward from the place she was and the things she'd glimpsed in the smoke.

It was the morning after she left Ogrothan that the nor'-easter blew itself out in the waking world, leaving behind light variable airs barely strong enough to set the sails rippling. That was a frustration, since Cape Ann stood just visible on the horizon to the east and a good wind would put them home in a day. After breakfast the captain came over to Asenath and, with a formality that masked a long and friendly acquaintance, said, "Miss Merrill, maybe you can help us out a little. I don't imagine you want to stay out to sea any longer than the rest of us."

She beamed at him and said, "Sure thing." Half an hour later, after consulting the *Book of Eibon*, she stood just ahead of the railing at the *Abigail Prinn*'s stern with the thick humid air heavy about her, folded her fingers together in a complex pattern, held a certain geometrical pattern in her mind's eye, and murmured the words of one of the incantations that made Atlantis the master of the oceans in its day. A minute passed, another, and then a crisp breeze sprang up out of the sea astern and blew steadily. The first mate shouted orders, the crew hauled on lines and brought the sails around, and within a few minutes the *Abigail Prinn* was making headway toward port. That cheered her; the grave thanks she got from the captain and the grins from the crew did even more, and best of all was her father's nod and smile, and the quiet words, "Well done, kiddo." The one uncomfortable note was Robin, who gave her a wan look she couldn't read at all and headed belowdecks.

Still, she had little time to worry about that as Kingsport Head loomed up and the *Abigail Prinn* swung past the North Point lighthouse and sailed up into the mouth of the Miskatonic River. Once they were on the river Asenath had to hurry belowdecks to get her luggage ready, and then stayed there as the schooner swung round the bend in the river just downstream of Arkham, slipped past the island with its lines of standing stones, and came to rest at the old quay on River Street. Once the steward came by to tap on the cabin doors and call out "all ashore," she got Rachel safely tucked into her shoulderbag and hurried up onto the deck, located her father, went down the gangplank with him, and headed up the long hill beside him toward the familiar front door of 638 Powder Mill Street.

Once inside there were the usual things to say and do: a hug for her mother, who spent most of her waking hours in a wheelchair now and whose curling brown hair had a little more silver in it than when Asenath had left Arkham in June; a casual greeting from her brother, who barely looked up from the big leatherbound book on transcendental chemistry he was reading; and an odd little bobbing motion from a clawed and tentacled creature in a hooded robe, to which she replied, "Hi, Pierre. I missed you too." The parlor didn't seem to have changed at all, the couch and chairs and bookcase were still where they had been, but everything had the faint familiar strangeness she recalled from past years, the sense of returning to a place that was not quite what it had been.

Lunch was fish chowder and homebaked bread and raw fish dipped in familiar sauces, with a big pitcher of water that had proper sea salt in it. By the time lunch was over the wagon had come up from the quay with their luggage, and that had to be unloaded and hauled to various destinies—clothes to the laundry room, suitcases and chests to the basement, her books and keepsakes to her bedroom—and once that was done, Asenath plopped on the couch with her mother and recounted what she'd learned from Betty Hale that summer. She talked about Cassie's appearance and disappearance, too, for Laura Merrill was the Grand Priestess of the local lodge of the Esoteric Order of Dagon and knew a great deal about the old lore. She felt a pang of disappointment when all her mother did was shake her head and say, "That's really quite strange. I'll ask around and see if anyone else knows anything about it."

Later still, as night deepened over Arkham, Asenath gave her customary goodnight kiss to each of her parents and climbed the stairs. As the familiar steps creaked beneath her feet, she thought of all the years she'd climbed those stairs to bed, and all at once thought of how few years remained before she would leave 638 Powder Mill Street for a home of her own. The thought left her feeling troubled, and she tried to push it out of her mind.

CHAPTER 6

THE GARDEN OF THE IMMORTALS

"A lot of memories to let go of," said Owen Merrill. Asenath gave him a doleful look, knowing he was right.

They stood on what was left of a beach facing southeast toward the blue reaches of the Atlantic. Waves rolled up onto the sand, always different and always the same, but the landward side had changed. A scattering of pine trees killed by the rising salt water stood there, pale as ghosts, and so did masses of gray stone left behind by some long-departed Ice Age glacier.

Asenath could still remember the days when the trees were green and the stones flanked the trail to the private beach the Chaudronnier family owned, north of the Miskatonic River's mouth and south of the long-abandoned Wavecrest Inn. Now the gray hulk of the inn was gone, pounded into splinters by winter storms and washed out to sea, and the beach had been driven back by those same storms until just a dozen yards of sand dotted with stones and dead pines remained between the surf and the cracked and crumbling road to Arkham. Only the soaring mass of Kingsport Head, blotting out a third of the sky to the south, seemed unchanged.

"I know," said Charlotte d'Ursuras. Brown-haired and round-faced, she looked comfortable in jeans and a loose yellow blouse. "Father thought it was worth having one last clambake here before the beach goes away, and it seemed like a good idea to me."

A dozen paces along the beach, in a space free of dead pines, a fire crackled and blazed, tended by two more people Asenath knew well: Martin Chaudronnier, the stocky gray-haired patriarch of one of the old Kingsport families, and Charlotte's husband Alain d'Ursuras. Tubs of clams and other seafood and baskets of vegetables sat on the sand nearby, waiting for their destiny in a pair of big cast iron pots. Off past them two children sat on the sand, Sylvia and Geoffrey d'Ursuras, twelve and eight respectively. An absence Asenath could feel hovered around them: their older sister Emily, Asenath's closest friend since before either of them could walk, who was spending a year in France with relatives.

That wasn't the only absence that weighed on Asenath just then, and she turned away, walked down to the edge of wet sand where waves rushed and flowed away, listening again to the voices of the sea. Her mother had stayed home—her wheelchair bogged down in sand too easily—and Barnabas had begged off, pleading a book he wanted to finish; Asenath knew the real reason, which was that he had Aspergers syndrome and didn't like social events. Robin's father couldn't go out in sunlight without getting sick, and so Robin and his stepmother were throwing an indoor party for him as they always did at summer's end; Ms. Kendall the music teacher would be there, Asenath knew, along with an assortment of friendly shoggoths and various other friends who didn't like sun and salt water. The Shrays had a Tcho-Tcho ceremony that evening, too, so it was just the Chaudronniers and a few others, there at the last.

Memories tumbled through Asenath's mind as she stood facing out to sea: golden Kingsport summers of her childhood, when the big clambake on the beach marked the day before the long drive back up to Dunwich for the school year; more recent summers after they'd moved down to Arkham, and then the last few years when she'd spent summers in Chorazin studying witchcraft with Betty Hale and the clambake welcomed her back home. Always there had been children rushing into the surf, Deep One relatives swimming up to greet them, friendly faces, a sense of timelessness in the pleasures of the familiar. It stung to realize that she'd already seen the last of those bright and laughing days, and that the curtailed fragment of it around her would close off that set of memories once and for all.

As she stood there, watching the waves and feeling glum, an obscure sound rose slowly above the rush of surf. Eventually it became the noise of tires picking their way unsteadily over crumbling pavement. Asenath turned, startled, and her face lit up as she spotted something yellow moving off past a line of still-living trees in the middle distance. She hurried up the beach and through the dead trees to the edge of the road just as a battered yellow Toyota grumbled to a halt there.

"Hi, Dr. Akeley," she said as soon as the doors opened. "Hi, Aunt Jenny. I'm so glad you could both make it."

"I wouldn't miss it for the world," said Miriam Akeley, who was tall and thin and silver-haired. "Hi, Sennie." She finished extracting herself from the car and went to the trunk. The other simply smiled and gave Asenath a hug. Jenny Chaudronnier was "Aunt Jenny" to Asenath, though they weren't related by any tie of human blood; short and plain, with a mop of unruly mouse-brown hair, she was the greatest sorceress of that age of the world and one of the fixtures of Asenath's life, by turns confidant, wise elder, and instructor in arcane lore.

As other voices called out greetings, Asenath went to the trunk and helped Dr. Akeley carry more food and drink down onto the beach. By the time she'd finished with that, her father was deep in conversation with Jenny—they'd walked a short distance away from the others—and Dr. Akeley was talking with Martin and Alain. Asenath glanced them both, decided that she was going to enjoy herself no matter what else happened, and flopped down on the sand next to Sylvia, who gave her a quizzical look and then asked a question about Barney.

They chatted for a while; after that, Asenath talked with Dr. Akeley, mostly about kyrrmis; later still, as the fire burned down, things got quiet, and Asenath guessed that the others were thinking about past clambakes and summers long gone, the way she'd done earlier. After a while Jenny turned away from the fire, where she'd been standing, and went to one of the big rocks. Middle-aged though she was, she scrambled up on top of it without difficulty and perched there, looking out to sea.

Asenath considered her for a while, and abruptly decided that the clambake had gotten too serious. She went to another rock next to Jenny's, scrambled on top of it, and sat there facing the same way Jenny was. After a long moment, she said, "Yop."

Jenny looked at her, visibly startled, and so did Dr. Akeley, who'd left the others to come that way. Asenath looked away and put an innocent expression on her face. Jenny regarded her for a time, then turned back to face the sea and said, "Yeep."

Asenath stifled a laugh, and kept gazing out to sea, while Dr. Akeley looked on with one raised eyebrow and Jenny waited. At last, Asenath said, "Yoop."

Jenny started laughing then, and Asenath laughed too and let herself slide down onto the warm sand. "Somebody's been reading the *Book of Eibon*," Dr. Akeley observed. "But this isn't Saturn, and neither of you makes a very convincing Djhibbi."

"Why not?" Jenny said, still laughing. "Plato said that human beings are featherless bipeds, didn't he? That's close enough."

Dr. Akeley chuckled and shook her head. Down the beach, the fire finished sinking down to coals, and Asenath scrambled to her feet and went to help fill the kettles.

* * *

The next Monday was the first day of classes at the Starry Wisdom parochial school. Asenath tried to settle back into the familiar rhythm of the school year, and managed it at first. Familiar faces and new subjects of study kept her distracted for the first weeks of the term, though in quiet moments she brooded over Cassie's appearance and disappearance. Not that many days passed, however, before she returned to the puzzle in earnest.

After classes she sometimes went to the downtown Arkham public library to look up something for an assignment. One day, as the silence of the old brick building wrapped around her like a comforting blanket, she went there to research some events in Arkham's past for a history class. That meant reading old newspapers, and the public library still had the huge bound elephant folio volumes of back issues of the Arkham *Advertiser*.

It took her a little searching to find the one with JUNE 1898 in faded gilt letters on the spine, but she wrestled the big folio off the shelf, carried it over to the nearest table, opened it carefully and began turning the pages, revealing stories on long-forgotten local news from Arkham and the little towns around it. One of them stirred a whisper of memory: a man named Royce H. Arden was going to give a lecture at the Arkham Chatauqua Hall on Boundary Street titled "The Yellow Peril: China, America, and You." Asenath rolled her eyes—she knew enough about American history to recognize that first phrase, with its heavy cargo of ignorance and fear—and then stopped, because the article mentioned the Kuen-Yuin. She glanced at the speaker's name again, and a sudden suspicion took shape.

The fiction stacks were close by, and Arkham's connection with H.P. Lovecraft meant that the library had a respectable collection of classic weird tales. A few minutes later she'd found a Robert W. Chambers anthology that had "The Maker of Moons" in it, and moments afterward she'd confirmed her guess: the viewpoint character in that story was named Roy Cardenhe, and that name was a simple anagram of Royce H. Arden.

She sat back, then turned the pages of the newspaper volume gingerly to the day after the lecture. Sure enough, an article about Arden's talk filled most of a page in the local section. She started reading it, and found words she knew well by then: the city of Yian-Ho, the alchemists of the Kuen-Yuin, and Yue-Laou, the Dzil-Nbu of the Kuen-Yuin. A little further down she found a few words about a man named Frank Harris who'd died hunting the Kuen-Yuin, and she didn't have to look back at "The Maker of Moons" to identify that name with the Franklyn Barris of the story. She turned to a new page in her notebook, scrawled notes as quickly as she could, and then noticed a date at the bottom of the article and went to get another volume of the newspaper.

More than two hours passed before she got home, and by then she was late for her share in making dinner and had to stumble through an embarrassed apology to her mother. Laura seemed preoccupied, though, and as she and Asenath went to work in the kitchen, she said, "Your father just got a message from Maine. He's going to have to go there with your Aunt Jenny." In a low tone: "It's the Radiance again."

Asenath kept her reaction off her face. "How soon?"

"As soon as they can find a ship."

"I'm glad this is going to be a really good dinner, then."

That earned her a smile. "That's the spirit."

Neither of them had to say anything else. For longer than Asenath could remember, her father had gone away every so often, sometimes with others, sometimes on his own, hunting for the lost lore that might wake Great Cthulhu from his sleep or trying to stop some project of the Radiance. Neither of those were without risks, and Asenath knew every time her father went away that he might not come back. It was simply one of the things she'd learned to live with, though sometimes when he left she locked herself in her bedroom and cried, and other times she let herself daydream about what it would be like when Cthulhu rose from the sea at last.

That night, though, she did neither of those things. Instead, she opened the notebook she'd taken to the library and tried to piece it all together.

The Kuen-Yuin, she thought. The story said they were alchemists and sorcerers from China, and the lecture by Arden agreed with that. The story said they'd come to upstate New York to make gold, and Arden said they were in America. The story and the lecture both talked about Yian-Ho, about Yue-Laou, about a strange being called the Xin, and about a man who'd gone to hunt down the Kuen-Yuin and hadn't survived.

Somehow, too, it connected to Cassie, who'd appeared out of nowhere and vanished into thin air, and who knew about Yian-Ho. Asenath felt sure of that. Maybe it was pointless curiosity and maybe it was something to keep her mind distracted so she didn't worry about her father, but she decided she didn't care. She wanted to know more, and there were places in Arkham she might be able to do that. Tomorrow, she thought, and turned back to her homework.

* * *

"Dr. Whipple," Asenath asked, "do you know where I can find something about an organization called the Kuen-Yuin?"

The old man at the desk regarded her with a look she couldn't interpret at all. "That's a name I haven't heard in a good many years," he said. "And I'll need to ask why you want to know about it, of course."

The two of them, alone for the moment, were in the Van Kauran Reading Room, the restricted-collections room of Miskatonic University's Upham Library. Oak bookcases lined the square room's walls and long oak tables gathered in the center; Whipple's desk sat to one side. Above, clerestory windows let in the gray light of an Arkham autumn. Two years back, Asenath had finally earned the right to climb the long brown stair, make a certain pattern of knocks on the door to gain entry, and read such tomes of eldritch lore as her parents, her teachers, and Abelard Whipple agreed she was old enough and well enough instructed to study profitably. Someday, she knew, if she did everything she was supposed to, she'd have the run of the collection, but it rankled a little that for the time being, she still had to get permission each time.

"Did my dad tell you about the girl who showed up out of nowhere on Elk Hill?" she asked him. When Whipple nodded: "A lot of things she said and did are also in a story by a man named Robert W. Chambers, and that story mentions the Kuen-Yuin. I think it's supposed to be from China, but Chambers said they had people in upstate New York, and I found an article in an old newspaper that says the same thing." Whipple's expression didn't change at all, and Asenath went on with a growing sense of unease. "Dad and Aunt Jenny are off on another trip and I don't know anyone else who knows anything about this sort of thing, so I wanted to see if I could find out anything by myself."

Whipple regarded her. Was that a hint of amusement in those bright blue eyes? "I see," he said after a moment. "I imagine you've looked for clues elsewhere."

"Well, yes. I found a few things in the public library, but that's all."

"That doesn't surprise me." He unfolded himself from his chair and started for the shelves along one wall. When Asenath gave him an uncertain glance, he motioned with his head, indicating that she should follow. As they crossed the room, Whipple said, "Friedrich von Junzt wrote about the—" The words that followed were in Chinese, so quick and fluid that Asenath could only just parse them.

She gave the old man an uncertain look. "Is that the Kuen-Yuin?"

He glanced back at her. "Yes. You know how hard it is to write Aklo words in our alphabet, I believe. Chinese is similar—and of course it doesn't help that the different Chinese dialects pronounce the same word differently. These days it's usually spelled Quanyuan Hui." He spelled the words out for her. "But the 'Q' stands for the sound we write 'Ch' in English. When I was an undergraduate, we wrote the same words Ch'uan-yuan Hui."

They stopped by one of the shelves, and Whipple pulled down a volume bound in black cloth, with faded gold lettering on the spine. THE BOOK OF NAMELESS CULTS, it spelled out, and Asenath's breath caught, knowing that she was about to have the chance to read one of the most famous of the old tomes.

"The Quanyuan Hui had yet to leave China in von Junzt's time, but he stayed in Hong Kong and Kunming before his journey to the Plateau of Leng, and met with them in the latter city, I believe. You'll find his account in chapter twenty-nine." Then, indicating the book: "The Golden Goblin Press edition of 1909. The publishers insisted on cutting nearly a quarter of von Junzt's text, but the chapter you want was left intact. I can allow you to read it—but you'll have to promise me that you'll only read that one chapter."

She'd expected the restriction, gave the promise, followed him back to his desk and borrowed a pair of white cotton gloves from the stock he kept in one of the desk's few unlocked drawers. Then, equipped with a pencil and a spiral notebook with slightly yellowed pages, she perched on a chair at one of the big tables and opened the book to the page he'd named.

CHAPTER TWENTY-NINE, the heading read, THE KUEN-YUIN. Below that were a dozen paragraphs on von Junzt's voyage from the ruins of Nan Madol on the island of Ponape to Hong Kong, and his journey by land from there to the city of Kunming in the southern mountains of China. After that came two pages about his dalliance with a Eurasian woman called

Ysonde. Asenath rolled her eyes, turned to another page, and found what she was looking for:

> The next day Ysonde led me through a warren
> of narrow streets to a hidden door in a tiled
> wall near the market, and then through wind-
> ing passages in utter darkness. How she saw
> our route I do not know, but eventually we
> came to a windowless room lit by flickering
> oil lamps. There I met Yue-Laou, the Dzil-
> Nbu of the Kuen-Yuin, an ancient Chinese man
> with skin like parchment and a long white
> beard. I repeated to him the words I had been
> given by the worshipers of Great Cthulhu
> in New Orleans, and he smiled and gave the
> answering words. Castro, the young sailor
> who guided me into the bayous, had told me
> that the leaders of the Cthulhu cult lived in
> the mountains of China; over the next hour,
> as I spoke with Yue-Laou and Ysonde trans-
> lated for us, I discovered that Castro had
> spoken the simple truth.

Her pencil darted over the notebook page for the next quarter hour or so, copying down what she wanted to know. The Kuen-Yuin had been founded around 1200, or so von Junzt said, bringing together what remained of several older secret societies dating back into China's distant past, and it worshiped gods Asenath thought she could name easily enough—Meng-Dju the Dreaming Lord, Hei-Yang-Mu the Black Goat Mother, Huang-Wang the Yellow King, Chan-Xen the Toad God, and more. Its members practiced sorcery and alchemy, and were revered throughout China as masters of the Tao. As for Yian-Ho, Yue-Laou mentioned it in passing, then dodged all von Junzt's questions about the city.

It occurred to her, as she turned another page, that Robert W. Chambers had probably read von Junzt and heard a talk by Royce H. Arden, and borrowed details for "The Maker of Moons" from those the way H.P. Lovecraft had plundered eldritch tomes in the libraries at Brown and Miskatonic for raw material for his stories. Had Chambers simply moved the story to upstate New York because Arden said the Kuen-Yuin were in America? It seemed plausible—and then she remembered that Cassie had vanished in the Cardinal Woods, not in the mountains of China, with a cry of "Stepfather!" that could have come straight out of the story.

A few minutes later she finished Chapter Twenty-Nine. The heading on the next page read CHAPTER THIRTY, THE PLATEAU OF LENG, and it took her an effort to close the book at that point and give it and the cotton gloves back to Abelard Whipple.

"Did you find what you were looking for?" he asked.

"I don't know," Asenath admitted.

"Well, there you are." Then, with a vague distracted smile that she'd long since guessed was pure disguise: "If there's anything else I can help you find, Sennie, why, do let me know."

* * *

"Aye, I know of 'em," said Captain Enoch Coldcroft. "Tea for ye?"

"Please," said Asenath.

The old man gave her an amused look, left the parlor. Asenath made herself breathe deeply. She'd know the Terrible Old Man for many years, and had visited him often enough with her parents or with Aunt Jenny, but she knew enough about him to know that he deserved the name his sailors had given him all those years ago. One time she'd seen the strange glass bottles with lead stoppers he kept in another room and, being a witch in training, realized at once what it was that he kept in them.

If she'd been able to think of anyone else in Arkham who might be able to answer her questions, she'd have stayed away, but Enoch Coldcroft had sailed tall ships to China and back, and Chinese was one of the languages he knew.

The parlor didn't look as though it had changed noticeably since the eighteenth century. Two comfortable wooden settles framed a cast iron Franklin stove that looked old enough to be from Ben Franklin's own workshop. On the side away from the stove and the fireplace behind it, a window of narrow diamond-shaped panes let in plenty of light but only the dimmest sense of the world outside. Great oaken beams crossed the ceiling, and gray flagstones paved the floor. Asenath thought she remembered that the little cottage on Sentinel Street had been rumored to be the oldest building in Arkham, and haunted to boot, when the Terrible Old Man moved up from half-drowned Kingsport and purchased it with a sack of gold doubloons.

Coldcroft came back, handed her a cup of tea—strong Chinese tea that smelled of tar and spices, mellowed with cream and sugar—and sat in the settle facing hers, a similar cup in his own hand. Woolen sweater and dungaree trousers made him look as though he'd just come from the sea, and his face, wind-tanned to the consistency of leather and edged with a white beard, revealed nothing. Eyes the unnerving color of aged gold regarded her. Asenath fumbled through words of thanks, tried to assemble her thoughts.

"The Quanyuan Hui," he said, before she could manage the feat. "That's their right name, though if I hadn't sailed the China run a good many times and learnt somewhat of their language, damme if I'd be able to tell ye as much. Why d'ye like to know about 'em?"

Asenath found her voice. "I saw some things this summer in Chorazin and the Cardinal Woods, and Dad found something in the woods—a little stone seal, the kind of thing that used to be called a chop. He said it might have been theirs. I don't know how they could have gotten from China to upstate New York, but I thought you might know if anybody did."

"Aye, that I do," said Coldcroft. "I ought to know, as it was partly my doing—mine and my crew's." He drank tea, leaned back. Asenath waited.

"I'd met 'em a long time afore," he said then. "When I was a young man and not half as wise as many, I signed on with a ship that sailed 'round the Cape o' Good Hope for the Indies. No need to tell all that befell me, but I chanced to do a good turn for an old man in the harbor district of Canton, and he taught me sartain arts of which I won't speak. But I took oaths to him and to sartain others, and now and then afterwards they sent word and I helped 'em as I could."

"So the year 1878 came 'round, and none other than Nyarlathotep himself came to me and told me to take a good ship and bring some folk from China back 'round the Horn with me to this part o' the world. The Quanyuan Hui knew hard times were comin' in China, and they'd heard from people o' theirs who'd come here already that some folk wanted to close the ports to the Chinese, as they did not so many years on. So it was then or never, and I sailed as soon as I could. We'd rough work to do, for the other side was watchful, and we had much ado to keep away from their ships at sea and their men on land. I heard tell that Yueh Lao himself had to take a hand in it, to keep our folk safe."

"Yue-Laou," Asenath said. "The Dzil-Nbu of the Kuen-Yuin."

That earned her a level look. "That's not a title too many know."

"I read it in von Junzt's *Book of Nameless Cults*," Asenath confessed. "Who—who was he? And what's a Dzil-Nbu?"

"I never heard tell what Dzil-Nbu means," said Coldcroft. "It's no word in the Chinese tongue, I'll warrant ye that. But Yueh Lao, now, that'll take some telling. Look at the Moon some night when it's at the full. Where we see a face, folk in China, they see an old man in a robe leanin' on a staff with a cauldron by 'im. In China they say that's Yueh Lao."

Asenath processed that, said nothing.

"But the end of it was we got away and made for the seas south past Australia where the winds blow straight 'round the world with no land to stop 'em. It was a good long while ere I came back to port. That was in Innsmouth, since your folk knew well how to keep 'em safe from the other side, and the folk out o' China went ashore there and I never heard tell of 'em again. Maybe the other side was waitin' for 'em once they left Innsmouth, or maybe some other thing happened, but if they're still about they've been quiet a long while."

Asenath nodded, sipped at her tea. After a silence, she said, "Do you know what the—" She stopped. "I'm not pronouncing the name right, am I?"

Amusement showed in the golden eyes. "No worse than many."

He repeated the name of the Quanyuan Hui, and she tried to copy the sounds and tones. "Do you know what that means?"

"Aye, but it means more things than one. If ye ever try to learn Chinese ye'll have a devil of a time with words that sound alike. Hui means a band o' folk who've taken an oath together—our word 'league' ain't too far from right. But Yuan, write it one way and it means beginnin' and write it another way and it means garden, and Quan means perfect but it might also have somewhat to do with what they call an Immortal, which is a good bit more'n someone who doesn't get around to dyin'. So Quanyuan Hui might be the League o' the Perfect Origin and it might be the League o' the Garden o' the Immortals."

"The Garden of the Immortals," Asenath repeated, and all at once realized what it might mean. "Is that in Yian-Ho?"

The golden eyes regarded her for a long silent moment. "That's not somethin' an old sea dog like me ought to know, and it's not somethin' the likes of ye ought to be askin' of. Go lookin' for such lore and ye might end up there, and gettin' back, that's no easy thing." He motioned at her cup. "More tea for ye?"

CHAPTER 7

THE SECRET OF DUNWICH

She went home so deep in thought that she walked past her own front door. Once she'd corrected that mistake, climbed the stair to her room, greeted Rachel and spent a while petting the kyrrmi and enjoying her company, she sat at the old wooden desk with Rachel on her shoulder, pulled out her notebook, and wrote down everything she'd learned from the Terrible Old Man. None of it pointed yet in directions that made sense to her, but she could sense something moving off behind the details she'd gathered, a pattern that connected it all; it reminded her all at once of what she'd sensed in the Temple of Tamash in Ogrothan, the feeling of an architecture of events spreading outwards further than she could see. Brooding over that didn't bring the pattern any closer to awareness, but it left her wondering about another detail that might tell her at least a little.

That evening after dinner, when Barnabas had climbed to his attic laboratory to try one of the experiments from his book on transcendental chemistry, Asenath sat on the other end of the sofa from her mother and asked, "Mom, is it okay if I ask you a question about something that happened in Innsmouth?"

Laura's sudden smile was everything she'd hoped for. "Of course, dear."

"Back in—" She had to chase down the date in her memories. "1878, or maybe '79, some people came from China to Innsmouth. Did you ever hear anything about that?"

Laura was silent for a long moment. "Yes," she said at last. "Yes, I did. My great-grandmother Nora Eliot, who I knew when I was a girl, told me stories about her grandfather, who was one of the people who came from China. He was a young man, an initiate in the lowest degree of some Chinese order that worshiped the Great Old Ones, and he fell in love with an Innsmouth girl. There was some discussion between their elders and ours, she said, and everyone agreed that he would join the Esoteric Order of Dagon and stay in Innsmouth while the rest of them went somewhere else—New York City, I think. You could tell that Nora was part Chinese, too; she still had the little fold—" Laura's finger touched the inner corner of each of her eyes. "Right here. I wish you could have met her. You would have liked her stories."

By then Asenath had already grasped the point that mattered. "So I'm actually descended from somebody in the Quanyuan Hui." Laura gave her a puzzled look, and that meant Asenath had to explain all about the Kuen-Yuin from the story and the research she'd done. When she was finished, Laura nodded. "Yes, you are. Everyone in our end of the family is, and so are Matt and Sarah's end of the Waite family, and all the Eliots here in Arkham. I don't think anyone else remembers the name of the order Daniel Lee belonged to in China, though, so you've found out something that people will want to hear about."

Asenath blushed, promised to write it all down and to let her mother pass the word to the other people in Arkham who were interested in the history of vanished Innsmouth. Later that night, before she went to bed, she got out her notebook and wrote down everything her mother had told her, tried to make sense of the pattern.

They came here, she reminded herself. To Innsmouth, anyway, and then to New York City, where the Hudson River poured into the ocean. Follow the river north, with the Catskills on one side and the Taconics on the other. North of the Taconics you get to the Green Mountains of Vermont, and north of the Catskills you get to the Adirondacks and the Cardinal Woods. Was that where they went—and were they still there?

She knew better than to try to guess, and started getting ready for bed.

That night in her dreams she crossed the River Imro on a bridge of floating stones and climbed into the Tanarian Hills beyond. Broad slopes of grass and purple heather where great black bees hummed placidly stretched upwards before her, dotted here and there with low gnarled cedars in which breezes hissed. The grass was soft as moss, and she took off her boots and stockings so she could walk barefoot. Rachel made little pleased chuffing noises as they climbed, and Asenath glanced at her and smiled, knowing the reason: the kyrrmi liked Ooth-Nargai better than any other part of the Dreamlands.

Maybe halfway to the summit of the great ridge ahead of her, time quietly came to a stop. Asenath laughed. She always laughed when she reached Ooth-Nargai and felt time, weary with all its rushing, heave a sigh of relief and settle to a stop—or was it always the same laugh, as she entered a place where nothing ever changed? She knew better than to try to guess.

She kept walking up the slope, and in no time at all came to the crest. Below, bright in the distance, the soaring towers of Celephaïs glimmered in the golden light of an eternal spring. The snow-topped mass of Mount Aran rose beyond it, with the river Naraxa curving about the mountain's foot like a friendly serpent. Closer, gentle hills dotted with groves and gardens of asphodel, thatch-roofed cottages and the little shrines of the gods of dream. She had visited each of those shrines or would visit each of them, she could never be sure which.

Off in the middle distance, where a little cottage hid behind a nameless hill, she would find Miriam Akeley. In some sense not even the *Necronomicon* could explain, those who entered

Ooth-Nargai never entirely left it again; though Asenath planned on crossing the country to Celephaïs and taking ship there for Sydathria after what would be a few days anywhere else, she knew that she could always be found wandering the hills of Ooth-Nargai, and wondered why she never met herself there. The breeze brought no answers, and she walked on.

* * *

Her father's absence was palpable when she got home from school the next afternoon. Her mother had been busy with a class of novice priestesses all day, teaching them litanies, and looked so tired that Asenath took over making dinner even though it wasn't her day to cook. After the meal, Laura settled on the couch with a baby blanket she was crocheting for the Romeros two doors down, who had a child on the way, but dozed off before she'd done two rows. Barnabas had his nose deep in his book on transcendental chemistry, and Asenath knew perfectly well that he'd be unable to concentrate on anything else until he'd finished it.

That left only one option she could think of, and the next day before classes she ducked into the library of the parochial school and found Robin there, hunched over his math homework at one of the library tables. She considered him briefly from across the room, then crossed to the table, pulled out the chair opposite his without making a sound, and sat in it.

He glanced up a moment later, startled, and said, "Hi."

"Hi. Are you free after school? I need a card reading if you're okay with that."

"Sure," he said at once.

"Thank you, Robin. The Japanese Garden, maybe? I've got money for pretzels."

That got a quick smile. "You're on." A momentary pause, and then he went back to work on his homework. A glance at the clock told Asenath their first class wouldn't start for twenty minutes, and so she pulled out her second-year Aklo textbook and tried to force herself to concentrate on the grammar of a language not sprung from human brains and tongues. As she puzzled over the declensions of *fhtagn*, Abelard Whipple's comments about Chinese came to mind, and it occurred to her that she'd heard something like the name of the Quanyuan Hui before, but the memory proved elusive.

Classes and conversations with friends distracted her thereafter, but she met Robin on the steps in front of the school that afternoon. They found other things to talk about as they wove through Arkham's streets, heading north and east to where the tree-crowned mass of Hangman's Hill rose up steep above gambrel roofs, orange and red with the gathering autumn. Upton Park spread around the hill's foot; the playground, the splendid old Looff carousel with its painted wooden sea creatures, the white pillared bandstand beside Hangman's Brook, all of them had been familiar to Asenath since childhood.

Near that was the Japanese garden, a little labyrinth of winding paths and bridges flanked by twisted pines, flame-colored maples, tall gray stones dotted with lichen, and an assortment of benches and picnic tables. The two of them stopped at the concession stand near the carousel. Asenath bought the promised treat—two big soft pretzels dipped in salt—and from there they wove their way along the winding trails of the garden, found a picnic table in a secluded corner beside a cluster of old gray stones, sat there.

"This is about Cassie," Asenath said. She'd wondered how Robin would react to that, was relieved when he simply nodded. "I'm still trying to figure out what happened, and I thought maybe your cards can tell me something."

"Do you want to tell me what you know first of all?"

She nodded. "You heard what happened in the Cardinal Woods, right? Here's what I found our since we got back." Between bites of pretzel, she set out what she'd extracted from the Chambers story and the pages of von Junzt, what she'd learned thereafter from her mother and the Terrible Old Man, the few guesses she'd made, the many questions that still hovered about her memories of Cassie and an afternoon in the Cardinal Woods.

When she was finished, he waited for a while, and then pulled a cloth packet out of one of his pockets. Untied and unrolled, it revealed a set of cards with the Elder Sign on the back. They still looked new—the Starry Wisdom Press down in Providence had only started printing them a few years back, taking the designs from a copy with an older and stranger origin—but Robin handled them briskly, cutting and shuffling the deck three times, and then dealt three cards in a stack, turned them over, and fanned them out.

"The Broken Glass, the Coffin, and the Book," he said. "That's how it began. Loss, death, and a secret." He pondered the cards for a while. "Not just a single loss, either, not with the coffin and the glass next to each other. Plans failed, people died, and there's a secret that connects them somehow." Asenath nodded slowly.

He dealt three more cards, turned them over. "Lightning, the Clasped Hands, and the Mouse. That's how it came to you. A surprise, a meeting with someone, and then—gone."

"Cassie," said Asenath.

He glanced up. "I think so." Three more cards formed a neat stack on the table; he turned them over and spread them. "The Rider, the Moon, and the Railroad. That's what comes next. Someone's coming to meet you, someone you don't know about—there's something you don't know yet, too, but you will. The railroad means a journey. I can't tell if you're the one who's going somewhere, but somebody is."

He repeated the process. "The Dog, the Mountains, the Key. That's where it goes. There's someone you can trust, and that's good, because the Mountains always means trouble, something you have to face. Get to the other side and there's the key to the whole riddle. And then…" A final set of three cards joined the others. "The Rod, the Clouds, and the Star. The Rod means quarrels and misunderstanding. The Clouds might be the reason for the misunderstanding or it might be something else that gets in the way, but the dark side's toward the Rod, so it's probably a real mess. There's a way through it, though. The Star means there's a chance. Nothing's certain, but—" He shrugged. "A chance."

She thanked him, and he grinned. "Tell me what happens, okay?"

Asenath was about to agree when second thoughts intervened. "If I can, sure."

He gave her a dismayed look, and though they talked for a little longer, it felt to her as though neither of them was quite responding to what the other was saying. When neither could think of anything else to say, they fumbled through goodbyes. He left at once, disappearing around a bend of the trail a few yards away, and she stood there by the table, looking off toward fallen ginkgo leaves floating in a nearby pond and feeling bleak. For a little while she'd felt the same sense of familiarity she'd shared with Robin back when they were still children, and it stung to have that taken away again.

A moment later she heard footsteps coming back toward her along the path. Robin? She thought so at first, but the sounds were too light, and seemed hesitant. The idea of having to face some stranger dismayed her, but she put on a smile she didn't feel and turned.

Then she saw who was approaching, and her mouth fell open.

"Hi, Sennie," said Cassie.

* * *

She was still wearing the clothes she'd had on the day they had gone into the Cardinal Woods, and a spray of hemlock needles in her hair looked as though it had dropped onto her moments before she'd reached the stone circle. Something else had changed, though: the frightened air she'd had about her had vanished completely.

A moment passed before Asenath managed to speak. "Hi." Then: "Are you okay? How did you get here?"

"I'm fine, but I'm not supposed to tell you how I came," said Cassie. "But my stepfather wants to talk to you, and you can ask him. Will you come with me?"

"How are we getting there?"

She covered her mouth with one hand, stifling a laugh. "On our feet. It's just a little way further into the park."

Unnerved, Asenath still nodded, and followed Cassie's lead up the trail a little and then along a narrow path of smooth flat stones that wound its way in among a thicket of ginkgos. "How did you know I was here?" she asked Cassie.

"I'm not supposed to tell you that either." She sent an apologetic smile back over her shoulder, kept going.

The path veered around a small maple with flame-red leaves and reached one of the little hidden places the garden had in profusion. A thicket of bamboo shut out the view from one side, the rugged slopes of Hangman's Hill blocked a second side, and on the third stood a rough slab of gray stone twice Asenath's height that looked as though it might once have belonged in a stone circle. A bench of concrete cast to look like stone waited on one side of the trail. Sitting on the bench, completing Asenath's confusion, was Dennis Cooper, the martial arts teacher from Cardinal Springs, who glanced up and said, "Good afternoon, Sennie."

"Hi." After a blank moment: "You're Cassie's stepfather."

"Yes. I'm sorry we had to lie to you and your father, but I had to make sure you were who you said you were. I've had traps set for me before."

"So has my dad," said Asenath.

Cooper's eyebrows went up, but he nodded. "First of all, I wanted to thank you for being so good to Cassie. You and the other people who helped her bailed us out of a really tough spot."

"I did something very foolish," said Cassie, sitting down on the path by Cooper's feet. "I left—the place I was—thinking I could get to a certain other place, and because I didn't know what I was doing I ended up somewhere I didn't know at all. I was scared out of my wits."

"I remember," said Asenath.

That got her a sudden smile. "You and Miss Hale were so very kind to me, and so was everyone else. The only place I knew for sure I could get back to where I came from was in the Cardinal Woods, and so once I could think again I said that was where I lived." With a little embarrassed shrug: "That wasn't quite a lie, because I did live there once for a while."

"Where did you come from?" Asenath asked her.

It was Cooper who answered, though. "Yian-Ho."

Asenath nodded after a moment. "Okay."

"I don't know how much you know about that city," Cooper went on. "Cassie tells me she saw you cast a spell on your father, so I'm guessing you might know quite a bit. But she also told me that you said you were born and raised in Dunwich, Massachusetts. Is that right?"

"Yes," Asenath admitted.

"I was born there too," said Cassie.

Asenath's eyebrows drew together. "I knew all the kids in Dunwich."

"This was a long time ago." Cassie met her gaze. "Time in Yian isn't like time here."

Outside of time as well as space, Eibon had written: Asenath recalled the Hyperborean mage's words clearly enough. "Cassie," she asked then, "when were you born?"

"Nineteen twenty-seven."

She glanced at Cooper, who said, "I wasn't there at the time. I'm Cassie's fourth stepfather. She's a responsibility I inherited, you might say. Not the only one, either, and it's time for me to take care of one of the others. That's why I wanted to talk to you."

Asenath said nothing.

"I know you've got no particular reason to trust me," Cooper said then. "I can give you one, but I'd like to let that wait for a bit. What I want to say now is that you might be able to help Cassie and me rescue someone who deserves a much better fate than he's had."

"Okay," said Asenath after a moment, and waited for him to go on.

It was Cassie who spoke next, though. "Sennie, my full name is Cassilda Whateley."

Asenath took that in, and then put the name and the date together in what she tried to tell herself was a wild guess. "Yes," Cassie went on—had she read the name in Asenath's face? "My father was named Wilbur Whateley. I think you've heard about him."

Just as Asenath opened her mouth to say something—what, she could never afterwards remember—the bells in the East Church steeple started tolling the hour. She looked up sharply, realized what time it had to be. "Cassie, Mr. Cooper," she said. "I—I think I want to know more about this, but I should be home by now. If I stay out much later I'm going to have to do a lot of explaining to my mom."

Cooper laughed. "No problem. Let's see—tomorrow's Saturday, right? Can you come here during the day? I can explain the rest of it."

"I can't be sure when I'll be free," Asenath said.

"Don't worry about it." His gesture dismissed the question. "Whenever you come here, we'll be waiting."

* * *

That night Pierre went downstairs to his basement room as soon as the dishes were done, and Barney lingered only a little longer before heading up to his attic laboratory, the big brown book on transcendental chemistry tucked under one arm. Asenath and her mother settled in the parlor. Two lamps cast a pleasant yellow glow over the familiarities of the room. Asenath tried to keep her attention on the chapter of the *Book of Eibon* she was supposed to be studying, but too many questions circled in her mind to permit that. Finally she looked up and said, "Mom, do you mind if we talk a little?"

"No, not at all," said Laura, closing the book in her lap. "I think I've read the same paragraph four times now."

Worrying about Dad, Asenath thought, and tried to push her own worries aside. "You know the story by Lovecraft, 'The Dunwich Horror,' right? What actually happened?"

Laura gave her an inquisitive glance, and Asenath said, "Somebody after school mentioned it, and I started wondering about that whole business, and why nobody in Dunwich ever said anything about it."

"It's something most people in Dunwich still don't like to talk about," said Laura. "You remember Emily Sawyer, right?" Asenath nodded. "She told your father and me the story after we'd been living there for a year or so. I think you're probably old enough to hear it now."

Asenath nodded uneasily, wondering what she'd stumbled into.

"It all began around 1880 with a man named Noah Whateley, who was a seventh-degree initiate in the Starry Wisdom, and one of the elders of the Dunwich church. He was married, and then his wife died, and he got married again to a much younger woman. He loved her dearly—and then she was shot dead by a negation team when the Radiance came." An old story, her shrug said: all the worshipers of the Great Old Ones knew that the enemies of Earth's ancient gods might strike at any moment. "Noah Whateley couldn't accept that and go on, the way we have to so often. He decided that he was going to find a way to hit back at the Radiance, hurt them even worse than he'd been hurt, and when the other elders of the Dunwich church tried to talk some sense into him he just got angrier. In the end he left Dunwich with their one daughter, and settled at a farmhouse a few miles out of town."

"The elders kept an eye on him, of course, but all they could tell was that he was doing rituals to invoke the Great Old Ones up on Sentinel Hill, and that wasn't anything out of the ordinary. Nobody knew that he'd found a couple of very rare books of sorcery somewhere and kept them secret from the elders. He had some very powerful and dangerous rituals, the kind that humans can't use—that only a child of one of the Great Old Ones can. So his first project was to get a child of Yog-Sothoth that he could raise and teach."

Asenath drew in a sudden breath, understanding. "Yes," her mother said. "His daughter Lavinia studied sorcery with him as she grew up, and in the end he shared all the details of his plans with her. She was willing, and once she was old enough—well, I don't think I have to go into the details. She had twins, Wilbur and Clifford, and Noah taught them both everything he knew, and poured all his own grief and anger into them. His health was failing by then, and he knew he wouldn't live to see his plan carried out. He died in 1924, and Lavinia died in 1926—nobody knows for sure what happened, but Emily thought she'd summoned something she wasn't able to control, and it killed her. That left the twins."

"This is where Lovecraft really made a mess of things. The two boys were twins and they looked it; they also looked mostly human—he made up the whole business about Clifford being gigantic and invisible because he thought it made a better story, and Wilbur wasn't anything like as oddly shaped as Lovecraft said. Wilbur didn't come to Arkham because he needed a book, either. He had all of his grandfather's books, and he corresponded with other sorcerers in this country and abroad, so he had all the lore he needed to carry out his grandfather's plan. No, he was lured here, and killed."

"By the Radiance," said Asenath.

"No." Her mother looked away. "By then he was doing things that couldn't be hidden, and he wasn't careful enough in some of the letters he wrote to other sorcerers, so word got out about what he was trying to do. Some of the Dunwich elders went to Providence to consult with the elders of the mother church, and they tried to come up with some way to make him give up his project without killing him, but—" Another shrug, helpless. "So they found some pretext to get him to come to Arkham, away from his brother and the protective spells his grandfather and mother had cast on the farm, and shot him dead."

Silence filled the parlor for a while. "What was he trying to do?" Asenath asked then.

"He was going to combine the Aklo Sabaoth with the Dho-Hna formula," said Laura, her voice low. "He was going to use the combined rituals to open a way for the beings of the outer voids to come to this lesser Earth, and let them loose on the Radiance."

Asenath stared, horrified. "But that's crazy. They'd wreck the whole world."

"I know." Meeting Asenath's gaze: "I don't think Noah Whateley cared. He was too caught up in his grief and rage, Lavinia adored him and wanted to help him get his revenge, and the two of them raised her sons to feel the way they did. The stuff Lovecraft put into his story about clearing off the Earth was made up, of course, but the results would have been closer to that than I like to think about."

Another silence came and went. "What about the other brother? What ended up happening with him?"

"Lovecraft made up nearly everything he wrote about that," said Laura. "There weren't any wrecked houses, and professors from Miskatonic University didn't go to Dunwich to patronize the local people and save the day. What Emily Sawyer said was that a few weeks after Wilbur died, Clifford Whateley went up to the top of Sentinel Hill and worked the Aklo Sabaoth the other way around, and went into the kingdom of Voor."

"The place where the light goes when it's put out," said Asenath, "and the water goes when the sun dries it up." Her mother nodded, and for a long while thereafter neither of them said anything at all.

CHAPTER 8

THE KINGDOM OF VOOR

She'd wondered while going to bed that night whether she'd keep her almost-promise to go back to the Japanese garden to meet Cooper and Cassie. By the time she woke, though, she had an answer. She'd spent the dreaming hours walking through timeless Ooth-Nargai, passing the little shrines of amiable gods that dotted the green and rolling landscape, with the towers of the city of Celephaïs and the high slopes of Mount Aran a constant presence. She'd stopped at a familiar cottage to greet Miriam Akeley, and talked with her about timeless things before going on. All the while the hints she'd gotten from Cassie and Cooper and the grim story she'd been told by her mother circled through her thoughts, and when she blinked awake to see dawn spreading gray and autumnal outside her bedroom window, she knew she had to go.

The morning went to other things—it was her turn to wash dishes after breakfast, and once that was done she went out back to help Barney and Pierre harvest another round of autumn vegetables. They finished a little after eleven, left a thank-offering on the altar to Shub-Ne'hurrath between the seedbed and the compost bin, and had plenty of time to put the tools away and wash up before lunch. Once lunch was finished, though, the rest of the day waited, and she turned to her mother and said, "Is there any reason I shouldn't go to the library and look up some things for my history paper?"

"None in the world," said Laura, and made a shooing motion with one hand. Asenath beamed, bent to kiss her cheek, wrapped herself in a coat to keep off the crisp wind, and headed out the door. The library was only a few blocks away from Upton Park, which made the fib she'd told easier to conceal but no less uncomfortable to think about. Still, she'd lived with secrets all her life and kept some of them even from people she cared about, and instinct warned her that what she'd heard from Cassie and Cooper wasn't the sort of thing to talk about freely. When I can, I'll tell Mom everything, she promised herself.

The wind sent leaves dancing down Arkham's streets and blew clouds across the sky, hiding and revealing the sun. The old town huddled in on itself, hiding its own secrets. Asenath thought of Dunwich, huddled in the little valley at Round Mountain's foot, where there were at least as many secrets as in Arkham, and where people she knew had doubtless spent the morning much the same way she had. She passed the downtown library and squelched a sudden desire to turn her lie into truth and go there instead of the Japanese garden. Ahead, Hangman's Hill loomed over the autumn foliage of Upton Park; she drew in a breath and went on.

Cassie was sitting on a bench just inside the entrance to the Japanese garden. She jumped up as soon as Asenath came into sight, ran over to her and said, "Thank you for coming back." They walked together through the garden's winding trails, past maples and twisted pines and old gray stones, and came finally to the same place where she'd spoken to Cooper the day before. He was standing over near the bench, and grinned when Asenath came into sight.

He motioned the two of them to the bench, then sat down on a flat stone over to one side, so his head was nearly level with theirs. "So," he said. "We talked about Wilbur Whateley yesterday. Tell me this. Did you go looking for information about him between then and now?"

"Yes, I did," said Asenath.

He waited for her to go on, nodded when she didn't. "Good. As long as you don't trust H.P. Lovecraft's version of things, you'll be fine."

Asenath decided to risk a small revelation. "I know. My mom's from Innsmouth."

His nod showed that he knew exactly what that entailed. "Okay. I mentioned yesterday that Wilbur Whateley kept in touch with other sorcerers. One of his correspondents was an old Chinese-American man who lived just outside of Cardinal Springs, New York."

Pieces of the puzzle fell into place suddenly. "Yueh Lao," she said.

Cooper's eyebrows went up. He regarded her, his expression otherwise unreadable, and then said, "I'm curious where you heard that name."

"A story by a writer named Robert W. Chambers," Asenath said. "Some things Cassie said reminded me of things in it, and I did some research after I got back here." All at once the half-remembered name of a martial art fused with words she'd read and heard in Arkham, filled in more of the puzzle. "You're with the Quanyuan Hui, aren't you?"

That got a moment of perfect silence, and then he nodded again. "You know quite a bit more than Chambers did."

"I read some books and asked some people."

When she stopped there, he allowed a smile and said, "But I haven't answered your question. Yes, I'm the League's current head in America. The man I mentioned, the teacher of my teacher's teacher, was the head of the League in his time. His name was Yang Xiaolong, but he's the one Chambers called Yueh Lao." Asenath gave him a puzzled look, and he gestured: who knows? "Yueh Lao was one of the titles of the founder of the Quanyuan Hui a little more than eight hundred years ago," he went on. "Probably Chambers found that out somewhere and decided to use it in his story."

Asenath nodded. "According to the records we've got," Cooper said then, "Wilbur Whateley wrote to Master Yang quite a bit, came to visit him twice, and spoke highly of him to Clifford. That's why Clifford wrote to him once Wilbur died, begging him to do something for Wilbur's daughter and her mother."

"Wilbur Whateley was a young man, remember, and there was a Dunwich girl named Amy Bishop who fell in love with him. When he died Cassie wasn't yet a year old and Amy had no place to go because her family had turned her out of their home. So Master Yang took her into his own home in the Cardinal Woods. But she was heartbroken about what happened, and she only lived for a few years after that."

"Did she know who was responsible?" asked Asenath.

"Everyone in Dunwich knew," said Cooper. "So did Master Yang. Do you?" When Asenath nodded: "That's what broke her heart. She knew why Wilbur died, and who did it, and why it had to happen."

Asenath considered that and glanced at Cassie. The girl met her gaze squarely, as though to say, yes, I know it too.

* * *

"So that was how Cassie ended up with the Quanyuan Hui," Cooper said then. "Of course it was a big problem in those days to have a white baby raised by anybody who wasn't white, so after a while Master Yang took her to Yian-Ho. That's something we know how to do, though it's not something you do lightly." With a shrug: "The Great Depression hit upstate New York hard, and a lot of people had to do a lot of scrambling to stay fed. That wasn't a problem in Yian-Ho, of course, and the people there—or the things you meet there that look like people—took care of her in their way."

"It's very peaceful there," Cassie said. "I used to play in the garden, or watch the birds, or just sleep for days and days and days on end, and they would bring me their kind of food and drink, and talk to me when I wanted someone to talk to. And people came to visit me there. Even my uncle came there sometimes."

"Clifford," said Asenath.

"Do you know what happened to him?" Cooper asked her.

"I know what Lovecraft said." Asenath considered him. "And I know what someone in Dunwich said about it."

"He went to the kingdom of Voor," said Cooper. "The spell his brother meant to use could be worked the other way, and he did that and stepped into the Unseen. Not to Yian-Ho—he didn't know how to get there, and I'm not sure he would have gone there even if he'd known how. He went very far, maybe farther than anyone else has ever gone, but the cycles of the kingdom of Voor brought him within reach of Yian-Ho from time to time. So he could meet Cassie now and then, and the masters of the Quanyuan Hui met him there too."

"You've met him," said Asenath.

"Of course. I don't think Master Yang ever went to see him in Yian-Ho, but Jimmy Yueh, who was my teacher's teacher, and Sam Gottlieb, who was the head of the Quanyuan Hui after Master Yueh and before me—they went to Yian-Ho to meet him, because by then we knew how the cycles ran. And of course all of us went there to check on Cassie, to make sure she was okay and to keep her from being drawn too far away from being human."

"Why didn't you just let her come back?"

It was Cassie who answered. "I would have come back a long time ago, but I wanted to wait for Uncle Clifford. He wants to come back too, and he can't do that by himself."

"That's an understatement," said Cooper. "For all practical purposes, he's trapped in the kingdom of Voor, and it's going to take serious sorcery, and a sorcerous artifact blessed by one of the Great Old Ones, to open the way for him and transform his body back into our kind of matter. At first we didn't have the sorcery, but after Nixon opened China in 1972 we were able to start sending people over there, claiming to be scholars, to do the necessary research. It took a lot of hunting, but twenty-odd years ago one of our people found part of the ritual in an old library in Hubei Province, and a few years after that we got the rest of it from an archive in Guangdong. Just last year we finally tracked down the artifact."

"Okay," said Asenath. "But there's still a problem?"

Cooper nodded. "Finding the artifact isn't the same as getting our hands in it. It's in a cave near Dunwich, guarded by spells and—something else. I've been there and so have some others. We've been able to learn something about the spells that guard it, and one thing we know is that they're the kind of magic that takes a virgin to unseal. Do you know about those?"

Asenath nodded, having studied that lore from two capable witches and the greatest sorceress of that age of the world. "It's the voor," she said. "The voor in the body has to be unmingled for some spells to work."

"Voor?" He gave her a blank look, then nodded. "Of course, you use the Aklo word. We call it qi, the breath of life."

"That's what I was trying to do," said Cassie. "To get to the cave by Arkham and see if I could get the thing that will let my uncle come back to earth. I thought I could go straight there from Yian, and found out only after I'd stepped through that I wasn't anywhere near Arkham. I don't know much about sorcery, but I wanted to see if I could do something."

At that moment Asenath knew exactly what they would ask her a moment later. To forestall a question she had no idea how to answer, she said, "Okay." To Cooper: "I've got two questions. First, you and the rest of the Quanyuan Hui have put a lot of work into all this, and I'd like to know why."

"That's fair," said Cooper. "Partly, Master Yang made a promise, and we believe in keeping promises.

Partly—" He grinned. "It's one heck of a challenge, you've got to admit." Then, abruptly somber: "But there's another thing. You read Chambers' story, about the guys who went up to the Cardinal Woods to kill as many members of the Quanyuan Hui as they could find. That actually happened, though Chambers changed the names around a bit, and it happened for the reason he said it did: we were doing a lot of alchemy back then, and word got out about the gold we'd made—we weren't as careful in those days as we are now. An organization I bet you could name was behind that, and they're still around."

"I know," said Asenath. "And yes, I know the name of the Radiance."

Cooper regarded her for a moment. "Your dad has had some run-ins with them, I bet." When she nodded: "So you know what they're like. They killed a lot of our people back in 1897, and we've got to worry about what might happen if they decide to send their goon squads after us again. Having somebody like Clifford Whateley back here and on our side would help—and he's agreed, if we can bring him back, to teach us what he knows about sorcery."

"Okay," she said again. "And why are you telling me all this?"

"A couple of reasons. First, Cassie saw you cast a spell, and—well, let's just say your father was really careful, but I can see things most people can't. He's some kind of initiate and so are you. All this time I've watched you paying attention to my thoughts, not just to my words." When she blushed: "I've been doing the same thing to you. But there's also this."

He reached into his pocket, pulled his hand out again, held it open with the palm up. On it was an ornate ring of dark metal set with twelve tiny red stones, glowing like sparks in a dying fire. Around the ring, hovering on the edge of vision, voor shimmered and flowed.

"I'm willing to bet," said Cooper, "you know whose ring this is."

A brief glimpse at a concert in Buffalo rose in her memory. "Nyarlathotep."

He nodded. "We've got a different name for him, but I know that one." Then: "He shows up sometimes—you probably know that. A week or so after you and your father rode with me to Fernville, he was waiting for me when I left the school in Cardinal Springs after locking up, and we talked for a while. He said that you can get the thing we need, if you're willing to do it. He also said the choice has to be yours."

* * *

The choice was hers. She reminded herself of that, even as she packed a big shoulderbag with things she might need and then sat at the old wooden desk in her bedroom while night gathered outside, and the old house on Powder Mill Street creaked and shifted in an autumn wind. Nyarlathotep's ring glittered on the desk beside her hand as she tried to figure out how to say what had to be said. Rachel, perched on her shoulder, watched in silence.

There was something else on the table next to Nyarlathotep's ring. Pale and ornate, the stone seal her father had found in the cabin in the Cardinal Woods stood there, its bottom end toward her, revealing ornate characters she didn't recognize at all. She'd tried to tell herself a dozen times, more, that she should take it back to the desk in her father's study and leave it where she'd found it, but intuition flared, demanding: it had to come with her. Her training had taught her never to ignore such promptings, but even so, it made her acutely uncomfortable to think of her father's reaction if he found out she'd taken it. She sighed, turned her attention back to the note she needed to write.

She'd thought at first of leaving a note on the kitchen table, but her mother slept poorly when her father wasn't there, and she needed to be sure there would be time to get well away from Arkham before anyone knew she had gone. That left one alternative.

> Robin, she wrote, I think you can tell whose ring this is. He wants me to help free someone who's in really bad trouble. I don't know how long I'll be gone, but I'll send word when I can. Please let my family know, and have them send a message to Dunwich to watch for me there. Thank you, thank you, thank you!—A.

That would do, she decided. Once the note was finished and folded, she tucked it into her shoulderbag along with the ring and the stone seal, made sure she had everything else she wanted to bring, and then said to Rachel, "You know you can't come with me. I don't know if it's safe to let them know you exist." Rachel made an unhappy noise, but clambered down from her arm onto the bed, gave her a sad look, and curled up on the pillow

Asenath thanked the kyrrmi, and then walked over to a corner of the room where she'd drawn certain lines and curves on the off-white plaster in violet paint. A gesture and an act of will later, the lines unfolded into a shrieking, roaring abyss of strange angles and looming prismatic shapes, which ended just as suddenly in a half-familiar bedroom: Robin's.

Moonlight through the window showed him sound asleep in his primary form, a softly writhing mass of pale tentacles half covered with blankets on a narrow wood-framed bed. The other items of furniture loomed up silent in the dim light. She watched him for a moment, feeling tangled emotions she couldn't name, then moved noiselessly to the place where he kept his dulcimer and set the note and the ring there, where he couldn't help but see it.

A moment later she was back in the abyss, and a moment after that she stepped out of a fissure between two boulders onto the top of a hill overlooking Arkham. She'd spent most of an hour calling to mind every spell she knew that might be useful in facing the unknowns of the task she was about to accept. Most of them could be done with nothing but the skills she'd cultivated, but there was one that would need something else. It took her a moment in the moonlight, searching the grassy summit of the hill, to find the herb she wanted: silver-gray and inconspicuous, with narrow leaves and tiny white flowers. She murmured a prayer, picked the narrowleaf thieveswort, tucked it into an inside pocket of her shoulderbag.

An instant later she plunged back into the abyss. It had taken her some thought to choose a place to come back into the world, since she didn't dare trust Cooper or Cassie with the secret of the power Phauz had given her, and an angle would make the transition easier. A buttress behind the old white bandstand in Upton Park met both requirements. An instant later she stepped out from behind it and walked toward the Japanese garden, where they had agreed to meet her. Her heart was pounding and her mouth felt dry, but she kept walking.

Moonlight turned the garden ghostly, painted the stones and trees in shades of pale gray and black. Cooper and Cassie were waiting for her just inside the entrance. They greeted her in low voices, and then Asenath said, "I'm ready. If you need help finding the road to Dunwich, I can help with that too."

"We're not driving," said Cooper. "You're going to get to see one of the things initiates of the Quanyuan Hui know how to do." His grin showed unnervingly bright in the moonlight. "Come on." He motioned for the two girls to follow, led the way deeper into the garden.

They stopped finally in the little alcove where Asenath had met Cooper twice. She gave him a puzzled look as he walked over to the big upright stone.

"This used to be part of a stone circle," he said then. "I don't know where or how it got here, but it's got the old enchantments in it." Without looking at Asenath: "What's solid here is an empty space in the kingdom of Voor, and what's empty space here is solid there. Did you know that? When a stone's been enchanted in certain ways, it can become a door." He turned then to face her. "When we get to what's on the other side of the door, follow me and don't let yourself be distracted by anything. Understood?"

She nodded, and he turned back to the stone, and took out of his pocket something small: a stone seal, Asenath realized after a moment, like the one her father had found in the house in the Cardinal Woods. Cooper pressed the end of it against the stone, and voor moved in unfamiliar ways, in the stone, in the world. All at once the stone opened up into infinite space.

"Now!" Cooper said, and stepped forward. Cassie followed, and Asenath went after them. For an instant she felt herself tumbling through limitless voids, and then all at once she stepped into the cool daylight of an unfamiliar morning, and she gasped in wonder.

"Quickly!" Cooper was already moving. Asenath made herself follow him, though she wanted nothing more at that instant than to stop and take in the scene around her.

They had stepped into in a garden where paths wandered between low shrubs of varieties she didn't recognize, and a golden sourceless light shimmered over all. Birds the color of blazing red sparks fluttered past, singing in high clear tones. Another bird, rose and gray in color, stood on tall legs on the other side of the garden and contemplated her with wise dark eyes. Past the low wall at the garden's edge she could see high-peaked roofs, cobbled streets, arched bridges the color of alabaster, great strange trees with flowers clustered on the branches, and hanging silver bells, thousands of them, chiming in the breeze. Off in the distance a vast conical mountain tipped with snow loomed over all.

"Here." Cooper stopped at a point in the garden that didn't seem any different than a thousand others. "Follow me."

He took another step, and Asenath followed—

And the garden vanished, plunging her again into limitless space.

* * *

Another instant, and she stumbled forward into cold gray light. She dropped to her knees on windblown grass, caught herself with her hands.

"Good," said Cooper. "That didn't take us as long as I thought."

Asenath, trying to clear her head, looked up. They were next to a standing stone on a hilltop she thought she should recognize. Clouds hid the sun, and the wind blew chill and damp. She picked herself up slowly, looked at Cassie, at Cooper, and said, "That was Yian."

"Yes. You're one of the very few humans outside the Quanyuan Hui who've seen it."

She nodded slowly, and then looked around. A slope covered by tangled grass and low herbs fell away before her, ending beneath dense forest. Further off, more hills rose up out of the woodland. A moment passed before childhood memories came back into focus and Asenath recognized the curves of the land: Round Mountain close by, Sentinel Hill a little further off. They were a few miles from Dunwich, a little above Cold Spring Glen.

Another moment passed, and she realized that the sun was well over to the west. Cooper's first comment finally registered. "How long did it take us?" she asked.

"Two and a half days," Cooper said. "Time flows differently there." He gestured down the slope. "Quickly, now." Asenath considered asking where they were going, but Cooper and Cassie were already walking by the time the thought formed, and she hurried after them

The route led straight down the slope to a little mountain creek, veered left to where stones allowed an easy crossing over the black splashing water, and then went further left, going alongside the stream on bare wet rocks through a narrow ravine between ragged stone cliffs dotted with moss and lichen. Maybe a hundred yards further the ravine joined a broader but equally steep-walled valley, and the creek splashed down over rocks to join a larger stream.

That was when Asenath realized they'd reached Cold Spring Glen. That wasn't a place Dunwich folk would go willingly; whispered stories hovered about it, as did wary silences that brought the stories abruptly to a close. She gave Cassie an uncertain look, but the girl hurried on after Cooper, toward the head of the glen and the looming mass of Round Mountain high above. Stifling her uncertainties, Asenath kept pace.

Another quarter hour or so and they reached the head of the glen, where steep slopes rose up on three sides. Low down, water streamed out of a mass of broken rock to feed the stream. Pines filled the glen, and in with them, not far from the spring, the roof of a small cabin showed black against the grays and greens of the slope beyond it. A narrow trail led toward it through rank and tangled grass.

"Okay, we're good," said Cooper as they came up to the little cabin. Weathered and sagging, its clapboard siding long since gone silver with age, it nonetheless showed marks of unobtrusive repairs, and the windows and roof were intact. "Did you ever come up here when you lived in Dunwich?"

Asenath shook her head. "No. Nobody went into Cold Spring Glen. I don't know why."

"There's a reason for it, and if everything goes well you'll get to see that a little later." He unlocked the deadbolt and pushed the door open. The single room inside was clean and dry, and the handful of chairs that furnished it looked recent.

"We bought this place a long time ago," Cooper said, "about the time the last of us got out of New York City, and it turned out to be close to the thing we need." He waved Cassie to a chair, turned to Asenath. "Are you up for trying to get it this afternoon? It's less than an hour from here, and I've got a map to show the way."

"I can do that," Asenath said. "How soon do you want to leave?"

A smile and a quick shake of his head gave her the answer she was half expecting. "You need to go alone."

"That kind of spell?" When he nodded: "Okay, that's worth knowing."

That got her a raised eyebrow. "So you really do know a fair amount about spells."

Asenath decided on another risk. "I've been studying to be a witch since I was eight."

He processed that, and smiled again. "Good. If you know anything that'll keep other people from seeing you, you might want to use it." In response to her questioning look: "I don't know that there's anyone watching, but it's better to be on the safe side."

"Okay," said Asenath. "I'll be back as soon as I can." Cassie smiled and nodded, but she hunched down a little in her chair as she did so. Asenath could all but taste the fear in her.

* * *

Outside the wind hissed through the pines, drove ragged gray clouds across the sky. Asenath glanced around, slung her shoulderbag from her left shoulder, considered the neatly drawn map Cooper had given her, and headed at an angle toward one side of the glen, where an old trail led upward. Knotted fingers and a few murmured words woke one of the spells she knew, a charm to mislead watching eyes. Then, remembering the herb she'd picked before leaving Arkham, she took her shoulderbag off her left shoulder and put it on the right, to baffle potential pursuit in a different way.

With those protections in place, she went onward, staying in the shelter of the pines. The map in her hand spelled out her route: up out of the glen by the narrow trail, westward around the flank of the mountain to a jagged mass of stone she thought she remembered seeing from the other side, and then up toward the peak. From there, it was simply a matter of finding the cave—if "simply" was the right word. There were supposed to be caves all through the region, but the only ones she'd ever seen in the years she'd spent in and around Dunwich were the shoggoth dwellings she'd visited down below Sentinel Hill.

She went on, pacing herself, and found the trail. It took some scrambling for her to get up out of the glen, but before long she clambered over the last steep place onto the mountain slope and glanced down. A back road from Aylesbury stretched out below her, a thin gray line half-glimpsed beyond trees. The ground was wet from rain and melted snow and the wind blew damp and cold, but her feet knew the texture of the land and she moved quickly.

A sound detached itself slowly from the wind: murmur in the distance, half-familiar from childhood memories. A car? She hurried toward a stand of pines, hid among them and watched. The sound grew louder, took on the shrill tone of an engine driven hard. A little later a small gray shape hurtled along the stretch of road she could see, fast enough that it skidded as it took the curve. It was gone moments later: headed toward Sentinel Hill, she realized. The momentary glimpse told her nothing about who might be aboard it, but even in her childhood it had been rare to see cars in the backroads around Dunwich.

She rose from her hiding place and hurried on once the car was out of sight. A glance at the map reminded her to round the curve of the mountain to the west, and the mass of rock was the one she remembered, a jagged outflung shoulder you could see from Sentinel Hill where the Dunwich people celebrated the seasons. From there her route led straight up the mountainside, rising out from among the pines into low shrubs and grass. She paused to catch her breath, spent a while looking toward Sentinel Hill, gauged the weather. That wasn't comforting—the clouds had thickened and darkened, the way they sometimes did before rain—so she got up sooner than she'd planned and set out on the last stage of the journey.

Finding the cave mouth wasn't easy. She had to press finger-tips to her closed eyes and murmur words in Aklo more than once to do it. That was a spell she'd learned from Betty Hale, one of many; it opened her inner senses to the way voor flowed up and down the landscape, pooling here, surging there, and folding in on itself at the place she needed to reach. Even with that help, the clouds had darkened further and a first few drops of rain had splashed down before Asenath scrambled up one more steep place, ducked around a low shoulder of rock, and found the entrance, a gash in gray crumbling stone facing westward, opening onto blackness.

Inside she could see little at first. As her eyes adjusted to the dim light, the space became visible: a rugged stone cham-ber with a floor that looked like packed clay. It wasn't a large cave, not much more than a single chamber with a few short passages opening off it, each one ending soon in masses of stone. She got a flashlight from her shoulderbag—she knew spells to see in the dark, but those took effort and the flash-light didn't—and searched the whole cave from floor to walls to ceiling. All the while, like a whisper echoing off the rock, the presence of something charged with potent sorceries reached her inner senses, but she could not tell where it was. She tried one spell, another, a third, without result. Nor did the beam of the flashlight show any hiding place or illuminate any clue in the cave that might point her in the right direction. Frustrated, she turned back toward the cave entrance.

Another problem greeted her when she reached the mouth. Those first drops of rain had turned into a steady gray down-pour, and as she watched, lightning zigzagged in the mid-dle distance, darting down upon a distant hill. The crack of thunder came moments later, shaking the mountainside. Even if she wanted to go back down to the cabin in Cold Spring Glen, she knew, she would have to wait until the storm finished.

The thought of searching the cave again occurred to her, but it seemed futile just then. Instead, she turned off the flashlight and sat down on the floor of the cave, far enough back from the mouth to stay out of the way of windblown rain. Lightning flared again, closer, and the thunder shook the air; she moved, found a place where an outthrust shoulder of the cave wall was smooth and she could lean back comfortably against it.

Rain drummed hard outside the cave mouth. Lightning flared again, more distant, and this time the thunder was a distant rumbling. Asenath, sitting there, wished that Rachel was there with her, curled up in her lap. She closed her eyes, let her head rest against the stone.

Just at that moment, footsteps sounded in the cave behind her.

CHAPTER 9

THE SECRET OF ROUND MOUNTAIN

S he looked back into the cave, startled, pulse pounding. A dim human shape stood in the shadows, not quite visible in the dim drowned light. A moment of utter stillness followed, and then a low hoarse voice spoke out of the darkness: an old man's voice, she realized after a moment, speaking English with an accent she couldn't place. "No need to fear me. I'll do ye no manner of hurt. Who are ye?"

"I'm sorry," Asenath said. "You startled me, that's all. I'm Asenath Merrill."

"Ah," the man said. "Me name's Giles Rowley."

"Pleased to meet you." A moment passed. "Do you live up here?"

That seemed to amuse him. "Nay, though I've stopped here some while."

The shadows of the cave hid all but a dim sense of presence, but she could hear him sit down, fumble with something, and then make the distinct t'ch-t'ch-t'ch of flint on steel. Sparks flew, caught on tinder; a faint reddish glow illuminated a lean face with a sparse beard, a thin-stemmed clay pipe. A little later a faint smell of tobacco reached Asenath's nose—not the rank odor of commercial tobacco but the dryer, subtler scent of the wild plant.

"I'll wager," said Rowley then, "that ye came by cause o' what this cave holds."

"Yes. Yes, I did—but I don't know what it is or how to get to it."

"No? How did ye come to hear o' the thing, then?"

"A man I met told me about it." Since more explanation was clearly needed: "A man named Cooper. He knows it's here, but someone like me has to get it."

"Aye, that's true enow." Rowley shifted. "Cooper, if he's the one I think on, I know him. Not the first to come here, though, not at all. There were Whateleys that were used to come here some while since to say their prayers to what's within, and others, too, betimes."

A silence passed. "Please," said Asenath then. "Can you tell me what's in the cave, and—and why I can't see it or find it?"

"Aye," said Rowley. "Or maybe. Tell me first whether it's by sun or moon or star that ye came to this place."

She considered him, startled. The words were signs of recognition, and she'd read them in old books, but centuries had passed since they'd been in common use among the worshipers of the Great Old Ones. It occurred to Asenath then that some of those books talked of groups that had gone into hiding centuries back. Was that the secret of Round Mountain? Was there some cult of the Great Old Ones older than the Starry Wisdom Church, hidden away in that corner of northern Massachusetts? She pushed the question aside, tried to recall the proper answer. "By the hornéd moon," she said. "Did you watch it set?"

"Nay," said Rowley. "Nay, but I pray I might see it rise."

She breathed a sigh of relief, knowing she'd said the right thing. "I hope you do," she said, though it wasn't one of the traditional signs. "I hope all of us do."

"Aye, may it be so," the old man said. "Listen, then. I can tell ye indeed of what's here and how it got here. 'Tis no pleasing tale, I warn ye."

A minute or two passed as he smoked his pipe. "D'ye know aught of a country called Greenland, north o' here a fair way by sea?" She nodded, and he went on. " 'Tis well. Long years ago a ship came there out o' Norroway, fleeing folk I could name, and aboard it was a chest bound all in iron, and a woman beside it to tend what was inside. In the chest was a bundle o' rich cloths, and in the bundle, so they say, a piece o' carven stone. The folk o' Greenland made the woman welcome, for they knew enow to give the same answers you did, and the chest and what was in it went to a hidden place north o' the Eastern Settlement. So they worked the rites and made the offerings, and the fish came to their nets and the grain grew tall and fair for them, as ye might know."

"But after years passed the folk I spoke of heard of it, and sent ships and men. It wasn't enough for them to find the thing, they meant to leave no one alive who'd known of it. So the folk of the Settlements died and so did any o' the old folk o' that country, the Skraelings as the Greenland folk called 'em, who lived too close by. But the ones who did that, they didn't find what they sought, it was too well hidden for 'em, and too well guarded by sorceries. So they sailed home afore winter came and left it behind."

"There were some few who'd stayed out o' sight the while, most of 'em Greenlanders but also one who'd come there from England on account of not wantin' to be burnt as a heretic, as the custom was in those days, and once the others were gone they went to see what could be done. Every boat had been holed and sunk, but they built a little craft from such timber as they found, and sailed away. They knew better than to think there was one safe place for 'em east o' the sea, but west, there were people who'd come over and made homes among the folk o' this land, and they thought to do the like. So they sailed, and went down the coast some ways, and came up into the mouth of a river—aye, the one ye can see not too far off from here—and the Misquat folk who lived in this land welcomed 'em and told 'em they could find others o' their own people if they went a deal further west.

"They went along the river, staying in villages o' the Misquats, but when they got upriver some deal they took sick, one after another, and died, and the last of all of 'em, the Englishman I spoke of, came this far and climbed the mountain to see his way, and then he took sick too. He found this cave for shelter from the rain, and he put the thing he'd brought out of Greenland at the back o' the cave here and worked spells around it to keep it safe from the other folk, and then he died too, and here it stayed.

"For there was a thing those that came here didn't know, and that was that the ones who'd killed the Greenland folk left somewhat behind 'em. What it was I know not, but it passed on the pox to such as touched it or came too close. That was what killed the ones who came from Greenland, and though they never knew it, the folk of each and every village took sick some deal after they left, and most died. And from the villages the pox spread all across the land. It wasn't the only plague that struck the folk on this side o' the sea, but it was the first, and one o' the worst of 'em."

* * *

Asenath tried to swallow, but her throat was dry. She drew in a breath and then said, "That's so horrible, that they did that."

"Aye. Albeit it's not the worst thing they've done."

"I know," said Asenath. "So the thing they brought—the carven stone—it's still here."

"Aye. The one who brought it here knew enow to call on Her that gave it power, and hid it thereby. Since then, some few folk who pray to the old gods were led here, and such as worked the old strong rites had such blessings of it as they wished and it had power to give. Albeit it's been no few years now."

"I bet," said Asenath. "There aren't many people living around here any more."

"That I know well," said Rowley. "And it's time the thing go from this place, to others who pray to the old gods. I've stopped here some while, as I told ye, waitin' for one who could take it to such folk."

"They pray to the Great Old Ones in Dunwich," said Asenath. "At the Starry Wisdom Church. You could have taken it there yourself."

"Nay." He drew on his pipe again. "That's work for other hands than mine. Ye know the way there, I'll wager."

"Yes," said Asenath. "Yes, I do, but I need to take it to Mr. Cooper first."

"That's well enow. I don't doubt he'll know what to do with it. As for the hidings, why, d'ye know the old prayer that calls to the Black Goat o' the Woods?"

"Yes. Yes, of course." With a smile she knew he couldn't see: "That's the first prayer to the Great Old Ones I ever learned."

"Aye? Wise of them that taught ye. Speak the words, call on Her, and ask what ye will. That'll find the door for ye. Openin' it, now, that's another matter, but if ye be the one who's meant to have it ye ought to be able. There's a thing with ye that can do what needs doing."

"Okay," said Asenath. "Thank you."

The old man refilled his pipe again, said nothing.

A silence passed, and the rain slackened. Somewhere in the forest below, an owl hooted. The sound sent shivers down Asenath's spine. Sitting there in the dimness of the cave, she remembered stories Betty Hale had told her about the early days of Chorazin, the epidemics that came through every few years, the Native American survivors who'd come stumbling out of the forest to the little settlement below Elk Hill and sat in stunned silence by Chorazin hearths, one or two left alive from villages of hundreds.

"I wish I understood," she said then, "why they thought they had to kill everyone."

"Oh, there was cause for it," said Rowley. "Their kind of cause, to be sure. In Greenland, in years long past, there was trouble for a time between the folk from Iceland and Norroway and the folk who lived there already, the Skraelings, but time passed and all of 'em found it better to live in peace. That's the thing those we're speakin' of couldn't bear. All the killin' and slavin' and stealin' of land and the rest of it, that was to keep a tight hold on this country and the people who came here, to stop 'em from learnin' from the folk here or the ones they brought over from Africa, to make well sure only a few might ever think to follow the old wisdom and raise altars to the old gods." The tobacco in the pipe flared red, casting a glow upwards onto Rowley's face. "None o' that had to be. Things might well have gone otherwise, here as elsewhere. Maybe they can yet, someday." Another flurry of rain drummed on the stone, and the owl hooted again. "Maybe."

* * *

Asenath blinked suddenly, rubbed her eyes. The rain had stopped, and light spread golden along the edge of the sky ahead of her as the clouds lifted and the sun moved west. She was still sitting at the mouth of the cave on Round Mountain. She blinked and glanced over to where Giles Rowley had been sitting, saw no trace of him. Well, of course, she thought. I must have fallen asleep while we were talking, and he went back to wherever he was staying inside when I found the cave.

Getting up wasn't easy, for she'd stiffened with the cold, but she managed it and went into the cave, calling out, "Mr. Rowley?"

Echoes chased each other into the cave. Asenath waited a few moments and then went further in. Behind her, the sky brightened further, and she could see a little more clearly. No one was inside. She called out again, more uneasily: "Mr. Rowley? Are you in here?"

No answer came back. Baffled, she waited a little while, then decided it was time to act on the instructions he'd

given her, the promise she'd made. The old words came easily: "*Iâ!* Shub-Ne'hurrath! The Black Goat of the Woods with
a Thousand Young!" Then: "Grandmother, if—if it's okay,
I'd like you to take away the concealment spells and let me see
the hiding place Mr. Rowley talked about."

She could feel a sudden movement of voor. An instant
later, behind her, the sun reached a break in the clouds and
sent light streaming straight in through the mouth of the cave
into its furthest reaches. She could see, at the back of the cave,
something that looked like stone but wasn't. Someone had
shaped the voor of the place with consummate skill, she realized, and drew on some considerable source of power to do so.
She walked up to the barrier, mulling over which of the spells
she knew might serve against an enchantment that strong. She
could feel the pattern that had been shaped by the one who'd
come here, the way it held the power that had come cascad-
ing through him from the Black Goat of the Woods. Some simple thing would unravel it, that was the way of such spells,
but what?

A moment passed before she thought of the obvious thing,
and beamed. Her shoulderbag disgorged her copy of the *Book
of Eibon* and the narrowleaf thieveswort she'd picked on a hill
overlooking Arkham. She found the right page in the book,
pressed the herb against the not-stone and repeated the words
of the incantation.

Nothing happened.

She tried it again, just in case she'd mispronounced a word,
but the result was the same. Frowning, she put book and herb
back inside her shoulderbag and tried to figure out what else
might work. "There's a thing with ye that can do what needs
doing," Rowley had said, but that didn't seem to offer much
help. The narrowleaf thieveswort's the only thing I have with
me that has that sort of power, Asenath thought, and then
stopped, remembering the way that Cooper had transformed a
standing stone into a portal.

After a moment, she reached into her shoulderbag again, and got out the stone seal her father had found in the Cardinal Woods. If voor moved through it she couldn't feel it at all, and whatever spells went with it were utterly unknown to her, but she shrugged and decided to try the thing by itself. She held it the way she would to mark something with the characters on its end, and pressed it against the not-stone.

To her astonishment, voor flowed, sudden and shimmering, spreading outward from the point of contact. The not-stone in front of her dissolved. After an instant she could see the narrow stone chamber beyond it—and Giles Rowley.

There wasn't much left of him, just a few brown scraps of human bone over to one side, as though he'd lay down there long before and never gotten up again. A scattering of other shapes lay about them, mostly corroded or rotted beyond recognition, but two things Asenath recognized at once lay in among the bones, as though they'd been in a pouch or a pocket: a piece of flint sized for striking sparks off steel, and a thin-stemmed clay pipe, its stem broken.

Asenath stood there for a long moment, then nodded slowly, understanding who and what she'd talked with while she'd waited out the rain. She crossed to that part of the chamber and bowed her head over the bones, murmuring the words of the Esoteric Order of Dagon's ritual for the dead. Only when that duty was done did she turn away from him and look for the treasure he'd brought to the cave from Greenland.

It wasn't hard to find, partly because of the intricately patterned voor that streamed from it and partly because of the dull red glow the sun struck from its wrappings. Asenath went to the deepest end of the little chamber, crouched down and picked it up from the cave floor. The cloth that wrapped it was heavier than it looked, and it gleamed in a way the sunlight wouldn't explain. Only when she brushed dust off it did she realize that it had to be cloth of gold.

Voor blazed in and around whatever was inside it, tautly intertwined currents capable of shaping the world in ways she couldn't predict, but too many uncertainties still surrounded her to give her the time to learn more about it. She pulled her attention away from the bundle, tucked it into her shoulder-bag, and went to the mouth of the cave. The sky was clearing as the afternoon deepened, and she could see shadows beginning to gather in the hollows of the land—

And moving through those shadows, two cars, following the same back road from Aylesbury she'd seen from lower down the mountain, going the same direction as the earlier car she'd spotted, west toward Sentinel Hill.

She put the seal, the book, and the narrow-leaved thieves-wort back into her shoulderbag and slung the bag from her right shoulder, then twined her fingers together and mur-mured a protective spell. Then, as hidden from watching eyes as she knew how to make herself, she began to pick her way down the slope.

The sun slid further west as she descended. Nothing else moved around her but the wind. The familiar landscape woke childhood memories, reminded her of times when the world had seemed so much simpler. Someday, she thought, someday when I've finished my training and gotten ready to work as a witch, maybe I'll come back here, to Dunwich or one of the other mountain villages, to heal people and animals who need it, tell fortunes, summon helpful spirits and chase off harmful ones. All at once she could imagine herself as an old woman in a little house like Betty Hale's, living by herself except for a kyr-rmi, busy with the little concerns of a little community, as shel-tered as anyone could be from the terrible forces that had flung Giles Rowley across the ocean and cut his life short so terribly.

But was that what she wanted? The question hovered before her, unanswerable.

It took her a quarter hour or so to descend to the jagged shoulder of rock she remembered, the one flung out toward

Sentinel Hill. From there she retraced her path around the mountain to the north, staying out of sight in among the pines. Her shoulderbag weighed on her arm, reminded her of the secret thing she'd found—and the ones who had gone hunting for it in Greenland all those years ago, and killed everyone they could find who might have known of it.

They'll kill me, too, if they find me. The thought wasn't new to Asenath, but it had a sharper edge to it than before.

She went on. A fold of the mountainside ahead, edged with pines, marked Cold Spring Glen. She angled her route to a rock that marked the path down to the cabin, and then stopped cold. Someone stood by the rock, facing her, waiting.

A frozen moment passed before she recognized the figure as Dennis Cooper. She hurried over toward him, experienced a momentary puzzlement when he didn't react to her presence at all, then realized that she'd forgotten about the protective spells she'd cast. She came closer, switched her shoulderbag to her left side, and released the other spell. His start of surprise when he suddenly saw her a few yards away made her struggle to suppress a grin.

"You're good," he said. "Were you able to get it?"

"Yes. It's in here." She tapped the shoulderbag.

"Excellent. Here's the bad news." Low and intent: "Someone's following us. I don't know who, but there's a way we've got of finding out if somebody's on your trail, and—yeah."

"I saw cars on the road," Asenath said.

"Some of those might be friends. I sent a message to the other members of the Quanyuan Hui. The first one who got here took Cassie on to Sentinel Hill, and the others are heading that way, but we can't risk waiting for them—especially with what you've got with you. Sentinel Hill's about three miles away and I know the route. Up for a hike?"

"Sure," she said, trying to keep her unease out of her voice.

* * *

In after years that journey through the woods northwest of Dunwich stood out in Asenath's memories as the strangest part of the entire adventure, vivid and intangible as a dream: two figures moving in near-perfect silence through the shadows of a twilight forest. At the time, though, it didn't resemble a dream at all. As she and Cooper hurried toward Sentinel Hill, Asenath's heart pounded and her nerves were on edge. Every stray sound and every glimpse of unexpected movement made her jump. The hill with its crown of standing stones seemed to back away from them as they pursued it, while afternoon deepened toward evening and the forest stretched on. Cooper paced ahead, seemingly tireless, while she strained to keep up with him. Her shoulderbag dragged on her left shoulder until the arm felt heavy and useless as lead.

It didn't help that more than once Cooper glanced sharply off to their left, where the back road from Aylesbury ran. He didn't say anything and she didn't ask, but his expression told her as much as she needed to know. Someone was coming along that road, approaching them: that was as clear as though he'd shouted it.

Time passed. Finally they came close enough to Sentinel Hill that it no longer seemed to be fleeing from them. Minute by minute, it loomed up against the darkening sky, until Asenath could no longer see the standing stones atop it, just the steep pine-clad slopes and the spur of rock that marked the beginning of the trail to the top. Off to the left, the fading daylight showed here and there between trees, marking the course of the road, but she'd listened carefully as they hurried on and never caught the sound of a car in motion. The possibilities unfolded themselves in her mind: either they were safe—

Or someone was already waiting for them. She knew she had no way to guess which of those was correct.

The hill rose up higher ahead, blotting out more of the the fading daylight. All at once Cooper motioned for her to stop, then leaned down and in less than a whisper said, "There's someone up ahead at the foot of the trail, and it's not one of my people. Not Radiance either, I think, but—" A quick shrug finished the sentence. "I want you to do whatever it was you did on the way down from the cave, and follow me. We're going to circle around so I can get the drop on him. No matter what happens, stay hidden. If worst comes to worst, take the thing you've got, get out of here, and go to ground."

Asenath nodded uneasily, then shifted her shoulderbag to her right side and twisted her fingers together to cast the concealment spell. Cooper's eyebrows went up sharply, and then he grinned and motioned for her to follow.

Most of the really big men Asenath had met couldn't move quietly even if they tried, but Cooper was an exception. Quick and agile as a cat, he picked his way through the woods, first heading away from the road and then curving back toward the hill and the beginning of the trail. She followed, wary and nervous, knowing that her spells would offer no protection if Cooper was wrong and the Radiance had sent one of its initiates to stop them.

They were most of the way to the foot of the hill when she glimpsed something ahead that wasn't a tree or a stone. Another few steps and she was sure it was a human being—brown-haired and dressed in a dark jacket and jeans. Something about the figure stirred a flicker of memory, but then Cooper moved ahead of her and blocked the other from her sight. A smooth noiseless movement extracted something gleaming from his coat pocket: a revolver, Asenath realized after a moment.

A pause, and then he stepped forward, raised the gun, and deliberately stepped on a fallen branch so that it broke with a snap. "Freeze," he said, his voice loud and hard.

Her heart pounding, Asenath stepped to one side so she could see what they were facing, and almost cried out.

Half a dozen yards away, at the foot of the trail that led up the hill, Evan Shray stood, looking back over his shoulder, his face startled but resolute. A big brown Alsatian dog stood by him, its fur bristling. In Evan's hand, his Tcho-Tcho knife gleamed.

* * *

"You," Evan said, his voice loud in the sudden silence. "You're Dennis Cooper, aren't you? What have you done with Cassie?"

Asenath didn't have to see Cooper's face to sense his surprise. "Who the hell are you?"

"That doesn't matter." He turned to face Cooper. "You were around when Cassie disappeared. I've got reason to think you were involved in that. My friend Sennie Merrill was trying to find out what happened to Cassie, and now she's disappeared too. I want to know where they are."

Asenath raised her hands to unweave the spell that kept her hidden. Before she could do that, though, Cooper nodded slowly, and put his revolver back in his pocket. "Okay," he said. "I think I know who you are. You want an answer to your question, though, you're going to have to earn it." A sudden movement, and he shed his coat. "You're holding that knife like you know how to throw it."

Warily: "Do you know how to catch it?"

"Try me," said Cooper. "You know the rules for this, don't you? You get an answer for every catch, and so do I."

Asenath moved to one side, out of harm's way. The Alsatian did the same thing. She gave it a startled look, then stifled a laugh, knowing who it had to be.

Evan raised the knife in the formal movement, point up, and threw it: a basic straight throw, easy to catch, testing an unknown opponent. Cooper caught it effortlessly by the hilt. "Where did you learn *fei dao*?" he said, and threw it back.

Evan caught it. "I don't know that term," he admitted. "What does it mean?"

The knife flashed between them. "Flying knife," Cooper said, raising the blade point up. "What do you call what we're doing now?"

"*Nga khatun*," Evan said, the knife in his hand again. "Where's Cassie?" He threw the knife back; it turned lazily in the air before Cooper caught it.

"Close by, and safe. *Nga khatun?* The Plateau of Leng's a long way from here." The knife flashed back toward Evan.

"Buffalo, New York's a lot closer." He raised the blade, paused. "So's Arkham, Massachusetts. Why are you hiding her?"

He threw the knife, and Cooper caught it. "Because I don't know if I can trust you, and I know damn well there are people who would gun her down without a second thought." The blade glinted in the failing light as he raised it. "So how did Tcho-Tchos get to those places?"

His throw was a more challenging one, but Evan caught it. "They came here as refugees after the Vietnam War. Where's Sennie Merrill?"

Another throw, another effortless catch. "Also safe, and even closer. And the Tcho-Tchos just up and taught you their martial art."

Even in the fading light, Asenath could see sweat on Evan's face; he caught the knife, but the movement was far from effortless. "My stepfather's Tcho-Tcho," he said. "I grew up in the Tcho-Tcho community. I speak Tchosi. So, yeah, they taught me. What do I need to do to get you to let me make sure Cassie and Sennie are okay?"

The knife flashed, rose point up in Cooper's hand. "We're sorting that out right now. Tell me this. You know the Tcho-Tcho language, you grew up with Tcho-Tchos. What do you know about the Dzil-Nbu?" He threw the knife.

Evan caught it with difficulty. "The Master in the North," he said after a moment. "There was supposed to be someone in the part of China just north of the Plateau of Leng who was friends with the Tcho-Tcho. They said that he was the master of some kind of order or society or something like that."

"Yes, he was," Cooper said, before Evan could ask his question. "And he is. He's the head of the League of the Perfect Origin, the Quanyuan Hui—and right now, in this country, that's me. I'm the Dzil-Nbu."

"You're lying!" Evan shouted, and threw the knife: a clumsy throw, and dangerous.

Cooper twisted out of its way and caught it neatly. He raised the blade, point up. "Tell me this. If I threw this back at you the way you just threw it at me, could you catch it?" Evan stiffened and blanched, giving him all the answer he needed, and he tossed the knife back, hilt first. "No, I'm not lying, and you know that. Sennie? You can show yourself now."

With a ragged sigh of relief, Asenath shifted her shoulder-bag to her left side and unwove the spell of concealment. Evan saw her and turned even paler; the Alsatian looked at her, too.

What might have happened next, she could not guess, but a voice she recognized at once came from just up the trail: "Stepfather, I—oh!"

Evan turned, fast, but not fast enough for Asenath to miss the sudden change in his expression or to fail to realize what it meant. "Cassie! Are you okay?"

She was a short distance up the trail, staring at him. "I'm—I'm fine."

"Cassie," said Cooper, "is this the young man you told me about?" She nodded. "I thought so." He turned. "Your name's Evan, right?"

"Yeah." Evan regarded him warily.

"I'm going to ask for your help, then. We're about to try to rescue Cassie's uncle, and it's not going to be easy."

"Evan," said Cassie. "Please."

If Asenath had any remaining doubts about what was going on, Evan's expression settled them. "Okay." Ruefully, to Cooper: "If there's anything I can do."

"You'll do fine," said Cooper. "I've got students who are better at *fei dao* than you are, but damn few." Then, with a glance at the other being present: "Is that actually a dog?"

"No, he's not," Asenath said, beaming. The dog gave her an irritable look.

Cooper turned to Cassie then. "You've got a message for me."

"Yes. I'm supposed to tell you that the Xin is here."

"Okay, good," Cooper said, visibly relieved. "We're safe, or mostly. Come on. We need to get up top as soon as we can."

"Go on up," said Asenath. "We'll be right after you."

Cooper considered that, nodded. "Okay. Stay on the trail and watch out for the Xin. If you leave the trail it might decide you're an enemy—and it's poisonous." He turned and started up Sentinel Hill, motioning for Cassie and Evan to follow.

CHAPTER 10

THE MAKER OF MOONS

Asenath watched the three of them start up the trail. When she turned back to where the dog had been, as she expected, Robin Martense stood there, dressed in loose colorless clothing she knew wasn't actually clothing at all, and giving her a bleak look.

"How did you and Evan get here?" she asked him.

"We rode our bikes," he said with a shrug. "About half a mile short of Dunwich we hid them in an abandoned house and I changed my shape so I could follow you by scent." Then, ruefully: "Evan thought you'd been kidnapped. I thought he might be right."

"Okay," she said. "No, nobody kidnapped me." All at once she thought of Giles Rowley and realized what his words would mean to Robin. "But I know why the people in Greenland died. I talked to a ghost on Round Mountain, where I had to get something, and the ghost told me what happened. He got there before Jan Maertens did. I'll tell you about it on the way up."

His face lit up, and then slumped again into the same silent withdrawn look she'd seen there so many times since summer's end. "Okay," he said.

Exasperated, she burst out, "Robin, for Father Dagon's sake, what's the matter?" Then, guessing what he'd say from his expression: "And if you say you don't want to talk about it I'm going to start screaming at you right here and now. Tell me."

His glance rose to her face, dropped again. "It's just—" He shrugged. "I know you're in love with Evan."

"What?" Baffled, she stared at him. "No, I'm not."

"Come on. The way you were talking about him in Buffalo after he made *yeng dakh*—"

"No," Asenath said again. "I'm not. And even if I was, which I'm not, I'd be wasting my time. Didn't you notice the way he was looking at Cassie?"

"Yeah," Robin admitted. After a moment: "He's been talking about her pretty much nonstop since we got back from Chorazin, too."

"I didn't know that," said Asenath. "Was that why he was so sulky on board the *Abigail Prinn*? He wouldn't talk to me either, you know."

He reddened, but nodded. "And you really aren't in love with him."

"Not even a little." She turned toward the trail, motioned for him to follow. "Come on. They're going to try to rescue Cassie's uncle and I want to help if I can."

"Okay." He started after her. "Who's Cassie's uncle?"

"Clifford Whateley, Wilbur Whateley's brother. Yes, *that* Wilbur Whateley. I didn't know it yet when you read the cards for me, but that's what I got tangled up in. That and what happened to Greenland and the Quanyuan Hui and a lot more."

"And the thing you've got in your shoulderbag," said Robin.

She glanced at him as they climbed the trail, weaving around ancient pines and outcroppings of gray stone dotted with lichen. "Can you feel it?"

"Yeah. It's something of Mom's, isn't it?"

"That's what the ghost said. I can't feel her energy as well as you can, you know."

They got to a steep place in the trail, and both of them had to scramble to get past it. Once they were on easier ground, Robin said, "So tell me about Greenland."

Asenath opened her mouth and then shut it again, because it had suddenly occurred to her why thinking that she was in love with Evan Shray had made him so upset. She swallowed, made herself think about Giles Rowley's words instead. "What—what I heard was this." Picking her way up the trail, now next to Robin, now just behind him, she repeated what she'd learned from Rowley. She had to stop more than once to go back and mention something she'd missed, and repeated herself more than once, because the whole time something giddy and dancing spun through her mind and pulled her thoughts into tatters. Somehow Robin didn't seem to notice. He nodded slowly, said nothing until she had finished, and then stopped suddenly and said, "I wonder what that is."

She looked past him, saw something crouched by the side of the trail in the grass. It looked a little like a crab and a little like a very large spider, but its body was covered with what looked like matted yellow hair, and eight little eyes like painted black dots gazed up at them.

"The Xin," Asenath guessed.

"And that means?"

She shrugged. "You'll have to ask Mr. Cooper. I think it's something that serves the Quanyuan Hui, or maybe they serve it."

There were more of the crab-things scurrying through the grass and the undergrowth, dozens or hundreds of them. None of them ventured onto the trail, but all of them seemed to glance up at Asenath and Robin as they moved past. "Come on," said Asenath.

A little further the pines gave way to bare ground and a circle of twelve tall gray stones, with another, low and flat, in the middle. Asenath blinked in surprise as she got there, because Cooper, Cassie, and Evan weren't the only ones waiting. More than thirty people stood by the tall stones, dressed in the kind of clothes she'd seen on outsiders who hiked and hunted; they ranged in years from teenagers to spry seventy-somethings and in ethnicity across the whole range that America had to offer, but all of them moved as though they practiced the same martial art that Dennis Cooper did. It occurred to Asenath after an instant that she was looking at the Quanyuan Hui.

"Okay, good," Cooper said, crossing to greet Asenath and Robin as they reached the hilltop. "Sennie, you'll have to introduce me to your friend." That got settled, and Cooper went on. "Is it okay if I ask if you've got any training in sorcery or, let's say, spiritual work?"

Robin shot a questioning look at Asenath, caught the signal she gave. "I'm a first degree initiate in the Starry Wisdom Church," he said.

Cooper's eyebrows went up. "That actually exists?"

"I hope so," Robin said, grinning. "Otherwise you better tell me where I've been on a lot of Sunday mornings and Wednesday nights."

That earned him a laugh. "Okay," said Cooper, and turned. "Jake? Tell Robin here what we're trying to do and how he can help." A lean sharp-featured man in his thirties crossed to them, took Robin back over to one side of the stone circle.

"Right over here," Cooper said then, turning back to Asenath. He led her to the other side of the circle. "This is my wife Lisa. She's our best ritualist—a damn sight better than me—and she'll be leading the ceremony while some of us make sure nobody interrupts it."

Lisa Cooper was a short stocky Chinese-American woman with round glasses and a ready smile. "It's good to meet you," she said to Asenath as they shook hands. "Cassie's told me a lot about you, of course. Let's get that relic put where it needs to be, and then we can talk through the ceremony and figure out what you can do to help."

* * *

Asenath had attended rituals at the Starry Wisdom Church and the Esoteric Order of Dagon lodge hall since earliest childhood, and the rhythms and movements of the quarter hour that followed were utterly familiar to her. In spare moments when she wasn't reviewing the ritual and preparing herself for the work ahead, she glimpsed Robin and Evan in different places outside the stone circle, listening intently to one of the older members of the Quanyuan Hui or going this way or that. It didn't surprise her, when the group divided into those who would be performing the ritual and those who would stand guard, to see Robin coming into the stone circle, while Evan headed outward with a group of others to watch one of the trails up the hill from below, and stop anyone or anything that got past the Xin.

She could tell when the last details were being settled and the last preparations made, too, from the way that movement slowed and tensions built. By then the low flat stone in the middle of the circle had a red cloth draped over it, two tall red candles on that, a brass bowl full of sand with a dozen incense sticks burning in it, and behind those, the bundle from Round Mountain. Asenath turned to face the bundle, ran through her part in the ritual one more time and then stilled her thoughts—that took more effort than usual, because Robin was not far from her line of sight and his presence kept on reminding her of the thing she'd realized on the trail upward. Still, she got her mind clear before the high clear note of a chime warned everyone to silence and stillness, and the rite began.

In the realm of the visible, not much happened at first. Lisa Cooper started chanting, her voice high and clear, repeating syllables in a language that sounded as though it might be the great-great-grandfather of Chinese. Others joined in the chant at intervals. Now and then Lisa went to the stone altar, picked up one of the incense sticks, and handed it to someone else, who took it, went to one of the standing stones in the circle, traced what Asenath guessed was a Chinese character in the air before the stone, and returned the incense.

It was in the realm of the invisible, the kingdom of Voor, that the real work took place, and Asenath could sense it clearly enough. The dark voor from deep within the earth and the bright voor from out among the stars rushed together, forming an intricate balance of forces around the wrapped shape in the center of the circle, the thing of Shub-Ne'hurrath's she'd brought from Round Mountain. More: at that moment she could sense the architecture of events she'd felt in the Temple of Tamash in Ogrothan, the vast moving shapes off beyond the sky, and knew that for reasons unknown to her, they all focused inward on that moment, that ritual.

The balance of forces stabilized, and Lisa Cooper, still chanting, walked slowly into the middle of the circle, cupping her hands together in front of her. Something like a spark blinked into being in her hands, cast a faint gleam up onto her face. The spark became a coal, a bubble of light, and then soared up to hover above one of the standing stones. It looked like the Moon, Asenath thought, or perhaps the Moon's younger sister come to visit the Earth.

The maker of moons, she thought then, remembering the story.

Another spark gleamed in Lisa Cooper's joined hands, grew and rose up to become another moon hovering over another standing stone. Another followed it, and another, and another, until each stone had a moon above it and the white glare made the stones and the hilltop and the people gathered there gleam like diamond.

They had told Asenath to wait for a signal, but she knew before Lisa Cooper nodded sharply that the time had arrived. The sorcerers of the Quanyuan Hui knew one set of spells for shaping voor and she knew another, but the moment the others began directing the flow of forces she could sense exactly what to do, twisted her fingers together in one pattern, a second, a third, murmuring the familiar incantations. Then she drew her hands apart sharply, pointed the first and third fingers of each hand at the glittering bundle at the center of the circle, and flung every scrap of will and voor and longing she could gather together into the work.

She could feel the combined forces surge, strain, tremble on the edge of failure. Then all at once they broke through, so abruptly that she nearly stumbled forward. In the air above the stone circle, a gap opened at right angles to every earthly direction. The moons unraveled into twisting shapes of light, and then went suddenly dark—

And in the near-darkness, lit only by the flickering red candles, something fell out of the gap in the air and landed hard near the center of the stone circle.

An instant of silence, and then Lisa Cooper's voice rose again, reciting an ancient spell of release. Twelve people took sticks of incense to the twelve standing stones and traced characters that had the same effect. The powers drained away as the architecture of voor dissolved back into the invisible. Then a flashlight clicked on, its pale yellow light almost absurd after the diamond glory of the conjured moons.

By that faint light Asenath could see Cassie dart out into the middle of the circle, toward a dim shape that lay sprawled there. "Uncle Clifford?" she said. "It's me, Cassie."

Another flashlight clicked on, and another. The added light gave Asenath a clearer look at the sprawled shape there: a man's body, stark naked and belly down on the ground, limp as a corpse. A sudden dread shot through her—had they succeeded only in bringing a lifeless body back from the kingdom of Voor?—but the head stirred as Cassie knelt by it, turning to face her. The fingers flexed a moment later, spread.

"Jake?" Lisa called. "Did you bring—"

"Sure thing." The sharp-faced man came out into the middle of the circle, a rucksack in one hand. "Can all the ladies please turn away for a couple of minutes? Thanks."

Asenath, blushing pointlessly, turned to face outward. Out beyond the stones, she could see little more than gathering night and the black shapes of the hills nearby against paler sky, but down below—only about two miles away, she remembered—the lights of Dunwich shone quiet and golden in the darkness.

* * *

"Okay," Jake said then. "We're good."

Asenath turned back inward. More flashlights clicked on, and by their light she could see the figure in the center of the circle: tall and lean, younger than she'd expected, with a mop of unkempt dark hair and a haggard, clean-shaven face. He was sitting on the ground, legs folded loosely, dressed in a sweatshirt and pants that were too small for him. He flexed and straightened his hands again, pondering them, as though not quite sure what they were. Cassie knelt next to him, facing him, her face alight.

Just then Dennis Cooper came into the stone circle. "No sign of trouble," he announced. "We might just have gotten away with this." He crossed to where Clifford Whateley sat and said, "Mr. Whateley? Welcome back."

The man looked up, and a first faint trace of a smile bent the harsh lines of his face. "Thank you." His voice, deep in the basso range, was rich with the old Massachusetts accent.

"Do you think you can stand up?"

"It may be a bit," said Clifford. "I ain't exactly used to this kind of body any more. Still, I know we got to leave."

Cooper nodded. "We're safe for the moment, but I don't know for how long. We also didn't know where you'd want to go or what you'd want to do once you got back, so—" He shrugged. "We didn't make much in the way of plans."

Clifford nodded. "I know where I ought to go," he said. "My only question's what they'll do if I show up there."

"Uncle Clifford," said Cassie, "I know someone who can tell you." She turned. "Sennie? Can my uncle ask you a few things?"

Startled, Asenath found enough self-possession to walk over to them. "This is Sennie Merrill," Cassie went on. "She grew up in Dunwich. She helped me when I went through the gate from Yian-Ho and ended up in the wrong place, and she also got the thing from Round Mountain we needed to get you back."

"Very much obliged to you," Clifford told her.

"I'm glad I could help," said Asenath.

"You know who I am and where I come from, I calc'late." When she nodded: "The thing I ought to do is go on down to Dunwich. If I've got any kin in the world other'n Cassie here, it's there or close by, and I want to know where I stand with 'em. Maybe you know 'em well enough to make a guess."

Asenath nodded. "Mr. Whateley," she said, "can I ask a question?" He gestured, inviting it, and she went on. "The spell that took you into the kingdom of Voor. You could have done it the other way around, the way your brother wanted to do, couldn't you?"

"Of course. If you can do it one way you can do it the other."

"Why didn't you?"

His eyes, dark and haunted, pondered her. "I asked myself that a lot more'n once. I know what Grandpappy and Mama wanted, and I know why. I watched Wilbur listen to 'em and take it all personal. I'm not sure why I didn't take it the same way, but I didn't. So when Mama died and it was just me and Wilbur, I tried to make him see reason, and so did the elders from Dunwich, and so did poor Amy Bishop—and when none of that worked, I did what I had to do. You see, it was me who talked him into going down to Arkham that last time, and I knew when he left that I wasn't never going to see him again."

Asenath swallowed, made herself nod. "Then they know that down in Dunwich, too. Mr. John Whateley's the senior elder now, and my dad says he's one of the best loremasters in this part of the world. He's got to know that you could have done—the thing your brother was planning—and you didn't." Then: "If you want to go to Dunwich now, I'll go with you.

Everybody knows me there. I can introduce you to the elders and tell them how you got back."

"You know," said Clifford, "I'm going to take you up on that."

A moment's silence followed, and then Cooper spoke. "I'm going to wonder out loud what the folks down in Dunwich would do if I came walking down the road with you."

Asenath turned to face him. "They'll be fine with it. I'll tell them that you worship the Great Old Ones too, and they'll welcome you. They did that when my mom's people came to Dunwich from Innsmouth eighteen years ago."

"Dennis," Lisa said, a short distance away. He glanced at her. "I hope you don't think you're going to go down there by yourself."

He assessed her, allowed a wry smile. "Apparently not." Then, to Asenath: "And if all of us come down with you?"

"I'll go in front," said Asenath. "Everybody in Dunwich knows me. I'll be out in front, they'll recognize me, I can explain who you are, and everything will be fine." She thought of Robin an instant later and turned, knowing there was something she could do to help heal the rift that had come between them. "Robin? Will you go in front with me?"

"Of course I will." He crossed to her side, stood there looking awkward.

"Robin didn't grow up in Dunwich but he's been there a lot," she told Cooper. "Everybody knows him too."

Cooper glanced at the others who gathered around them, dim presences in the starlit night. After a moment, he nodded. "Okay," he said. "I'm going to trust you. You should put the relic back in your shoulderbag; I'm going to guess they can sense that." He turned to Cassie and her uncle. "Mr. Whateley, would a hand up be any help?"

"I calc'late it would," said Clifford. Cooper reached out. Hands joined, and Clifford rose unsteadily to his feet. Only when he was standing did Asenath realize why the sweats he wore were too small: he stood more than six and a half feet tall, and towered over his niece and most of the others in the stone circle.

"Ready?" Cooper asked him.

He nodded and turned to Asenath. "After you, miss."

* * *

There were three trails down Sentinel Hill, but only one of them led straight to the path to Dunwich, and that was the one Asenath knew best. Memories clustered around every rock and old twisted pine that her flashlight beam touched, recalled holy days she'd celebrated on the hill with the Dunwich folk. She pushed those memories away, tried to keep her mind on the route and what she needed to say to John Whateley and the other elders.

Robin walked beside her or just behind her as the width of the trail permitted, and that set off another cascade of thoughts she had to shove out of her mind, most of them pointless variations on *he's in love with me he's in love with me he's in love with me.* Off past those moved something deeper and stranger. In a sudden rush of awareness she knew exactly what his body would feel like if it pressed close against hers. The thought made her blush furiously, but it remained, hovering and enticing.

She forced her attention away from that, toward the others who followed them. She could hear Cassie's quick quiet footfalls, Clifford's long but not quite steady pace, others. If she let her attention drift that way she could sense Evan close by and Dennis Cooper a little further back, in among others whose voor she didn't know well enough to identify. Outside the narrow range of flashlight beams, night pressed close.

The trail reached the hill's foot and veered not quite straight toward Dunwich, following the curves of the land. Flashlights stabbed forward past her, making her way easy to find. The lights were crucial, she'd explained to Cooper and the others;

they showed that the Quanyuan Hui didn't seek to take Dunwich by surprise. They were mirrored by the warm yellow lights ahead, oil lamps casting light through Dunwich windows—the little town had never had streetlamps and the electrical grid had gone out in that part of Massachusetts long before it failed further east. Flashlight batteries could still be had, but all at once Asenath wondered how soon those would stop being made—and what then? Lanterns, perhaps? Torches?

Irritably, she pushed those thoughts aside as well, kept walking.

It didn't take long to reach the first outlying houses of Dunwich, lined up on either side of an unpaved street. As she'd expected, there were half a dozen young men waiting, none visibly armed, and one of the elders, wiry old Tom Frye. He caught sight of her at the same moment she saw him, laughed, and then said. "Well, this is a surprise. Sennie, Robin, we got word to keep an eye out for you, but nobody said you'd be bringing friends."

She beamed. "Hi, Mr. Frye. I didn't know either—but yes, they're friends. Can you have someone go for John Whateley? There's a couple of people here he should meet."

Frye nodded to one of the young men, who made off at once. Turning back to Asenath, Frye said past her, "I'm going to have to ask the rest of you to wait just a bit."

"Of course," Cooper said, coming forward. "I'm going to guess your people have a dozen deer rifles or so trained on us right now."

Frye considered that, allowed a nod and a fractional smile. "About that."

"Sensible," said Cooper. "That's what I'd do."

Frye took that in, nodded again, and stepped forward to meet him. "Tom Frye."

"Dennis Cooper." They shook hands. "Ms. Merrill here hasn't said too much about Dunwich," Cooper went on, "but I get the impression we have some things in common."

Just then John Whateley arrived, a lean silver-haired man with thick glasses and the avuncular air of a small-town parson. "Well," he said, surveying the small crowd before him. "Good heavens. Sennie, Robin, good evening. The rest of you, good evening." Then, with a gaze turned suddenly sharp: "Sennie, what on Earth have you got in your shoulderbag?"

"Hi, Mr. Whateley," said Asenath. "I'll tell you all about that in a little bit. First I want you to meet two people I think are relatives of yours." She led him to Clifford and Cassie and said the usual things, introducing them.

John Whateley considered the tall man before him. "Clifford Whateley," he said. "That's a name that hasn't been heard much in Dunwich for a very long time."

"Since the spring of 1928 or thereabouts, I calc'late," said Clifford. "Yes, that's me, and Cassie here is poor Wilbur's child. These folks with us are the ones that helped us get back." He extended his hand, and John took it; some sign Asenath didn't know apparently passed between them, for John glanced up at Clifford's face and nodded.

"Sennie's quite correct," he said. "One of my great-grandmothers was Noah Whateley's youngest sister, so I believe that makes you my second cousin once removed—" He turned to Cassie. "—and you, child, are my third cousin. Well." With a slow broad smile. "I hope you'll both call me Cousin John. Now perhaps you can introduce me to your friends, and then we all ought to go somewhere a little less chilly than this."

At a quiet signal from Tom Frye, the young men moved unobtrusively out of the way. Asenath moved out of the way, too, while the introductions started, and Robin followed her, standing close but pointedly not looking at her. She watched him sidelong, saw half-hidden emotions tug at the corners of his mouth. And if he's in love with me, she thought, then—

Before she could finish the thought Evan extracted himself from the loose crowd around the Whateleys, the Coopers, and the two Dunwich elders and came over to her. He had a set expression on his face. "Sennie," he said when he reached her, "I want to apologize."

"It's okay." she told him.

"No, I mean it—"

"It's okay," she repeated. Then: "Does Cassie know how you feel about her?"

Even in the dim light, she could see him turn bright red. "Is it that obvious?"

She stifled a laugh. "Let's just say if your face gave things away in the *pauw* like that you'd get clobbered every single time."

Evan swallowed, and nodded after a moment. "Yeah. We've talked about it."

"Good. She's a really sweet person."

Just then Clifford and John Whateley began walking toward Dunwich's main street, deep in conversation, Cassie following them like a watchful shadow. Tom Frye and the Coopers started the same way a moment later, and the others began to follow them. Further into town, doors opened and people came out onto the street. Asenath watched them start and then turned back to Evan. "Do you know anybody in Dunwich?"

"Yeah, one of my stepdad's cousins married a guy from Dunwich a couple of years ago. You know Alan Sawyer, right? Do you know where he lives?"

"Sure. Two doors uphill from the Dunwich Inn Motel, same side of the street. The porch looks like it's got teeth and might bite you if you get close."

He grinned, thanked her and made off. She turned to Robin. "Come on," she said. "Unless you want to stand out here all night."

He looked at her then, gave her a rueful smile. "I'll pass."

They joined the ragged procession toward the center of town. Houses Asenath had known from the time of her earliest memories rose to either side, and beyond them stood other buildings just as full of recollections: the Starry Wisdom church, the public library, the general store, the school with the two big wooden pillars framing the main door. Even in the faint flickering light she could glimpse winters and summers past, the half of her life she'd spent in Dunwich and the many visits since she'd moved to Arkham. Her thoughts on Round Mountain about moving back to Dunwich surged up again, with a difference, for she knew with a sudden dizzying certainty that whether she moved there or not, she wouldn't be living by herself.

She and Robin had not yet reached the main street when a familiar figure came bustling up toward them. "Asenath? Oh, there you are. And Robin? Good."

"Hi, Mrs. Bishop," they both said. Suellen Bishop was the older of Dunwich's two witches, a short plump woman who habitually wore her silver hair in a loose bun.

"Yes, I've heard from both your families," she went on, as though they'd asked. "Martha Price got a message to me days ago, and I'll be sending something back to her as soon as the moon's up. Why don't you two come with me? It's not too late for dinner, which I'd be willing to bet you'll both want, and if either one of you forgot that I've got a couple of guest rooms, why, I promise you I haven't. And then some of the elders will want to talk to you."

They agreed, and then Asenath said, "I've got something I ought to give to the elders."

The witch smiled and nodded. "Of course you do, dear. You got it up on Round Mountain this afternoon, didn't you? A lot of us sensed that. Do you know what it is?"

"All I know is that it came from Greenland and it's bundled up in cloth of gold, and it belongs to Robin's mom and my grandmother. Did you know it was there?"

"Of course. I'd be a poor excuse for a witch if I couldn't sense it—but the Black Goat always said it wasn't time for it to come down from the mountain yet. I imagine that time finally came around."

"Do you know what it is, Mrs. Bishop?" Robin asked.

"Not yet. We'll find out later. For now, let's get some dinner and you can both tell me what happened." She motioned for them to follow.

* * *

"You're sure," said Suellen Bishop, standing by a kitchen table loaded with the remains of a hearty country breakfast: potato pancakes, applesauce, sliced ham, buttered toast. Around the table spread the familiar sights and scents of a Dunwich kitchen. "I can make more if either one of you is still hungry."

"If I eat one more bite of anything," said Asenath, "I'm going to rupture something." For his part, Robin made a little choking laugh and shook his head. The witch laughed, and crossed the room to close the vents on the woodstove.

Asenath leaned back in her chair and let herself relax. She had more reasons to smile than a good breakfast and the luminous autumn sunlight that spilled through the windows just then. While she'd slept, and traveled in her dreams further into Ooth-Nargai, Suellen had sent messages through the moon's rays and received some as well, and the last message from Arkham had an unexpected piece of news: Owen Merrill and Jenny Chaudronnier had finished whatever urgent task had taken them to Maine and were expected back home in Arkham within the week.

Robin was already gathering plates by the time Suellen came back from the stove, and Asenath roused herself from warm thoughts and started clearing the table as well. The next dozen minutes went into washing dishes and putting the kitchen back in order. They were maybe halfway through the process when Suellen said, "By the way, I hope the two of you didn't do anything you shouldn't, before you got to Dunwich last night."

Robin turned bright red and looked away. "No," said Asenath. Then, though she hadn't meant to speak the thought aloud: "That's for after we get married."

"Good. If you did, with the thing you had close by, there'd be a baby on the way for certain. I'm not sure what else it'll do, but it has that power."

To cover her confusion, Asenath made herself remember Giles Rowley's words. "In Greenland it brought fish to the nets and made the grain grow tall."

"I'm sure it did. If it stays here, why, we'll have more goats and chickens than we know what to do with in a few years."

Asenath laughed. "I know some hungry people in Arkham, humans and shoggoths both, who can help you out with that." The whole time she could feel Robin's gaze on her, startled and questioning, but she didn't dare meet it.

The last of the dishes got dried and put away, and Suellen dried her hands on her apron and said, "Now I need to do a few things before we go over to the church. Why don't the two of you sit in the parlor for a bit? I'll be right out."

Every witch's parlor Asenath had ever seen served as a consulting room as often as anything else. This one was no exception; it had a bookshelf of herbals and sorcerous tomes, an assortment of chairs and a sofa surrounding a low convenient table, a desk to one side and a cupboard full of herbs and charms on the other. Asenath went to look at the bookshelf, while Robin walked to the front window, looked out across the street, and said, "Wow."

Asenath glanced that way and then went to stand beside him. In the empty lot across the street where Dunwich schoolchildren played ball games during recess, the members of the Quanyuan Hui had gathered to practice. They moved in unison through an intricate form; the motions reminded Asenath more than a little of *khrang tayeng* moves. More than a dozen young Dunwich men leaned against the fence, watching them with obvious interest.

"You've studied martial arts," Robin said without looking at her.

She knew him well enough to catch what he wasn't saying. "I need to, you don't. I know what you can turn into." Memory brought back the one time he'd shown her: like his primary form, but with vital organs shielded behind a shell hard enough to stop bullets and each tentacle tipped with a hooked claw as sharp as a Tcho-Tcho knife.

"I've started learning another shape," he said after a moment. "I talked to Ms. Kendall last week and then went and talked to Sho, and so I'm learning how to turn into a shoggoth."

"No!" said Asenath, delighted.

"Yeah. Sho says I'm as clumsy as a brand new broodling but I'll learn."

"I'm jealous," she said then. "When I was a kid I used to wish that I could flow under doors and things the way they can."

He opened his mouth, closed it, and she drew in a breath. There was more she wanted to say, much more, and she was about to say some of it when the door from the kitchen opened behind them and Suellen Bishop came bustling into the room. "That's done," she said, "and they'll be finished soon at the church. Ready?"

The Dunwich Starry Wisdom Church a block and a half up the street was as familiar to Asenath as her own hands and feet. Its whitewashed clapboard sides, the humble wooden door in front, the plain pleasant worship hall inside, framed some of her earliest memories. She and Robin filed into the anteroom after the witch, made the sign and murmured the password of their degree as they passed into the worship hall, went up to the front and sat in the first row of pews, facing the offering table. A few others already sat alongside them, and nodded and smiled a silent greeting. Asenath responded in kind, leaned back in the pew and waited.

Others came into the worship hall, a few at first and then many more. Glancing back, Asenath was startled to see members of the Quanyuan Hui among them, but then caught sight of Dennis Cooper making the sign for the use of guests and guessed that one of the Dunwich elders had taught it to them. She thought about that, wondered what else might have been discussed between the League and the church the night before. Another stir of movement and she saw Clifford Whateley come into the church, ducking his head as he passed through the door; a flicker of movement half seen among other moving shapes told her that Cassie was with him.

The worship hall filled up, and the usual noises faded into silence. Then, for no reason that she could name, she happened to glance to her left, past Robin. Over to one side of the hall, leaning back in a folding chair, sat a long lean figure in black she recognized instantly. Eyes like polished stones met her gaze, and a finger that glittered with rings pressed against his lips, cautioning her to silence.

She was still staring at him when the chanting began.

CHAPTER 11

THE HERITAGE OF IREM

A senath, startled, looked toward the open doorway that led to the sanctuary. That was where the chanting came from, she was sure of it, but it wasn't any of the chants she knew from the Starry Wisdom liturgy. An instant later, catching herself, she glanced back to her left. The One in Black had vanished again—or had he? She couldn't see him there or anywhere in the worship hall, but a sense of his presence lingered, uncanny and unsettling.

The chanting grew louder, and finally Asenath recognized the words: a temple litany from the *Necronomicon*, one of the rituals that had invoked the Great Old Ones in the half-forgotten days before the seven temples were desecrated and the ancient gods of Earth bound for a time. Few people had dared to recite those chants in many centuries, and it astonished her to hear them repeated by voices she knew well.

Movement at the doorway resolved into Emily Sawyer, one of the Dunwich church elders. She wore a black ceremonial robe and had protective amulets tied on forehead and wrists, and she swung a censer on a long chain. The tang of incense spread through the worship hall. Another movement in shadows, and Tom Frye came into sight, also robed and protected with amulets. Two long poles rested on his shoulders, and he grasped them with his hands and moved with a slow, smooth pace. John Whateley came behind him, with the hindward parts of the two poles resting on his shoulders and gripped in his hands. Between the two of them, supported by the poles, was a boxlike shape, a portable shrine like the ones described in the old tomes. It was draped in cloth that glittered and flashed as the light struck it.

By then everyone in the hall was on their feet. Asenath stared and pressed her hands to her mouth as the two men brought the makeshift portable shrine over to the offering table as Emily Sawyer stood to one side, still swinging the censer. Anne Brown, another of the elders, came out last and went to the shrine once the men had stopped. She had silk gloves on her hands, and closed her eyes as she lifted a fold of the cloth of gold and reached inside.

She turned to set something on the offering table as the men took the portable shrine over to one side and set it down. A deep curtsey, and she backed away, but by then Emily Sawyer had taken her place, giving Asenath only the briefest glimpse at something small and black. The censer swung up and back seven times, filling the air above the offering table with pale smoke, and then Emily curtseyed and moved away. The elders stopped chanting a moment later.

The thing on the table was a a statue of a goat maybe a foot high, carved in black stone in an elegant style Asenath was sure she had never seen before. It reared up on its hind legs to show full udders, and the head was raised to brandish horns against the sky. Its square base had a line of unknown writing around it. In the statue and through it moved voor of an intensity she had never sensed before, and she didn't have to recognize whose image the statue bore to know why she'd imagined Robin's body pressed against hers so intensely, why Suellen Bishop had asked the question she had that morning, why Giles Rowley had spoken of grain growing tall. The power that made seeds sprout and beasts mate surged through it with overwhelming force.

She was still trying to process that when the four elders took up stations at the corners of the offering table, facing the statue. All together they chanted the ancient prayer: "*Iâ! Shub-Ne'hurrath! Black Goat of the Woods with a Thousand Young!*" An instant passed, and then most of the people in the hall repeated the same words: "*Iâ! Shub-Ne'hurrath! Black Goat of the Woods with a Thousand Young!*"

Asenath bowed her head then, and prayed silently: Grandmother, please bless me, bless Robin and Evan, bless Dunwich and everyone who lives here, and—and Clifford and Cassilda Whateley and Dennis Cooper and the Quanyuan Hui and—Names and faces tumbled through her mind, until she could only finish with: Please bless this lesser Earth and everyone on it. We need your blessing so badly.

Silence fell, and then gave way suddenly to the sound of a folding chair being moved. Startled, Asenath looked up, but the hands on the chair belonged to John Whateley, not to Nyarlathotep the Crawling Chaos. He brought the chair over to one side of the offering table, where he could see and be seen by everyone in the hall, and motioned for them to sit.

"Well," he said, sitting down. "Thank you all for being here. This is a very special day for all of us, but I'm not sure how many of you realize how special it is. Thanks to Miss Asenath Merrill—" He nodded to her, and she turned as red as her complexion allowed. "—and Master Cooper and the members of the League of the Perfect Origin, we've recovered something that I don't think any of us could have imagined."

"You all see the statue of the Black Goat; those who have the necessary training must feel the simply astonishing way that voor flows through it. Of course we noticed that when we took it out of its wrappings last night, and even more so after we worked the appropriate rites to th Black Goat to waken its power, but Emily Sawyer recognized some of the characters in the writing on the base, and it was a little past midnight when we found a certain passage in the *Necronomicon* that told us what this is."

"The writing is in Duriac, you see—the language of Irem."

A sudden murmur of low voices rose around her and fell just as suddenly still, but Asenath, hands pressed again to her open mouth, stared at the statue. She knew, just before he spoke, some of what John Whateley would say next.

"That sent us to a few other books—well, to be honest, we were up half the night in the church library. But the result of it all is that we know what the writing says, and so we know where this statue came from originally. It was carved in what we would call the year 1124 BC by the master-carver Etanna, consecrated by the high priest Utun-Abishu, and placed in one of the minor shrines of the Moon Temple of Irem."

He was silent for a moment, as though trying to fit his mind around what he had just said. "There were hundreds of statues in the Moon Temple, and thousands of other holy things. As far as anyone knew, most of them were destroyed by the soldiers of Alexander when the temples were desecrated by the Radiance, and the rest were hunted down in the years that followed—but one escaped. Whoever managed to take this statue and hide it must have been very careful indeed. I understand that it was in Greenland for many years, and before that in Norway; how it got there we may never know. But it's here with us now, and so we took the liberty of chanting one of the litanies that the priests and priestesses of Irem used in those days to worship Shub-Ne'hurrath. I don't imagine she minded that."

* * *

That afternoon, Asenath sat on one end of a sofa in Emily Sawyer's parlor and tried not to feel out of place. Dennis and Lisa Cooper occupied the rest of the sofa, and John Whateley, Emily Sawyer, and Suellen Bishop perched in chairs facing them. To one side, Clifford Whateley sat in a big armchair.

Someone had found or made a plain brown suit and a white shirt to fit him, and come up with a pair of shoes sized for his huge feet; a string tie, completing the ensemble, made him look like a young man from Dunwich gone courting in 1928. Sitting on the floor by his feet, wearing a cheerful blue and white checked dress, Cassie beamed impartially at all and sundry.

"We've got no claim on it," Dennis Cooper was saying. "Our lineage doesn't go back to Irem. Yueh Lao got his lore from the high priest of the great monastery of Leng, and according to our traditions it came to there from lost Sarkomand."

"We can certainly keep the statue safe here," said Emily Sawyer in response. "If your League ever needs to make use of its powers, though, please tell us. We're not likely to forget that it's because of you that we have it."

"That's very generous of you," Lisa Cooper said. "Likewise, if there's anything you need that we can provide, please let us know."

John Whateley said, "Why, there might be. I'm sure you saw how many of our young men were watching your people practice this morning. If you can teach your martial art to people who aren't members of the League, there's quite a few here who might want to learn it." His smile grew wan. "That might help the next time the Radiance pays us a call."

The Coopers looked at each other. "There are things we only teach to initiates," said Dennis, "but quite a bit of Quanyuan Quan can be taught to anyone who's willing to work hard. I have a senior student who might be interested in coming here." With a grin: "I saw him chatting up some of your young women earlier, so be warned."

"It wouldn't be the first time," said Emily.

"Does the Starry Wisdom Church allow its members to take other initiations?" Lisa Cooper asked then.

"I should hope so," said John. "Sennie here is an initiate of both the Starry Wisdom Church and the Esoteric Order of Dagon."

Dennis glanced at her, nodded. To John: "In that case we might be able to teach the whole system to at least a few of your people, if they're willing to take the vows of the Quanyuan Hui. We can work that out once we see who's interested." All at once he laughed. "This is quite something. A month ago I was sure I'd spend the rest of my life teaching in a couple of small towns way upstate in New York. Now I've promised Evan Shray to visit his teachers in Buffalo and Arkham, and if we set up a branch school here I'll be visiting regularly to keep an eye on things." Lisa smiled up at him, said nothing.

"Well, we'll be glad to see you here," said John. "Let me see. Is there anything else we need to settle now?"

"Not unless it's a problem that the Xin's back in Cold Spring Glen," said Dennis.

"Not in the least." John looked at him over his glasses. "What is the Xin, by the way? We knew there was something in Cold Spring Glen but I never heard much about it."

"It's a collective life form," Lisa said, smiling. "Like a bee-hive or an anthill, but related to horseshoe crabs rather than insects. We think it came from Sarkomand originally. There are three colonies we know of on this continent, the one in Cold Spring Glen and two up north of the Adirondacks; we take care of them and they protect us."

"Sensible of you. Perhaps we can discuss sometime whether it can help us out if things get difficult." He got to his feet and turned to Clifford and Cassie. "Perhaps I can introduce the two of you to Joyce now. I can't think of any good reason why the two of you should have to stay in the motel for another night."

Clifford nodded and extracted himself from the chair. Cassie, for her part, leapt to her feet and came over to Asenath. "Sennie, I know you'll be going back home soon," she said. "Will you come visit me here sometime?"

"Of course I will," Asenath promised. "And maybe you and your uncle can come down to Arkham sometime."

Realizing too late what that might suggest: "I promise you'll get a better welcome there."

"I'll keep that in mind," Clifford said with a wry smile. "Miskatonic University used to have a fine collection of books on sorcery. Do you happen to know if they still do?"

She beamed. "One of the best in the world. I can introduce you to the librarian."

A few courtesies later, the Whateleys left. Once they were gone, Asenath sent a questioning glance to Suellen Bishop.

"Oh, you hadn't heard yet, had you?" said the witch. "You remember Joyce Brown, of course. The poor thing's been living alone since her husband died in that accident out past the Devil's Hop Yard three years ago, and him so young, too. She's offered to give them a home and take care of them while they get used to being back in this world." With a sly look: "Unless I'm wrong, and I rarely am, he'll propose to her before the year's up and she'll say yes." She pulled herself out of her chair. "Well, we should be going now, I think."

"If you don't mind," Dennis said to her, "Lisa and I would like to talk to Sennie for bit first." The witch said something friendly and went out, and Emily Sawyer, taking the hint, went into the kitchen. Asenath turned to face the Coopers, uncertain.

"The one thing I still haven't heard," he said then, "was how you got the statue out from where it was hidden. Those were some robust spells you got past, and I heard that there was a spirit guarding them too. We'd like to know—if you're allowed to tell us, of course."

"Yes, I can tell you," said Asenath, "and you ought to know anyway, because it wasn't any of the things I know how to do that did it. It was something of—of yours, of the Quanyuan Hui's, I think: a stone seal my father found in an abandoned house in the Cardinal Woods. I don't know why it worked, but that was what did it."

The Coopers gave her baffled looks. "Do you have the seal with you?" Dennis asked.

"It's in my shoulderbag at Mrs. Bishop's. I can go get it if you want."

"That won't be necessary," said Lisa. She reached into her purse and extracted another seal, this one of fine-grained white stone. "Like this one?"

"Yes. Well, I can't be sure the writing on it's the same."

Lisa held it out, and Asenath took it. Lisa watched the seal intently for a moment and then said, "It's active," and held out her hand. Asenath returned the seal. "That's very puzzling."

"I'll say," said Cooper. "Normally you can't use the seal of Yueh Lao unless you're either an initiate of the Quanyuan Hui or descended from one."

"That explains it," Asenath said. "One of my great-great-grandfathers was a Chinese man named Daniel Lee, and I think he was a member of your League."

The Coopers looked at each other, and Lisa nodded after a moment. "There was a man named Li Dayuan who stayed behind in Massachusetts," she said.

"In Innsmouth?" Asenath asked.

"I don't know," said Lisa. "The records are lost. But it's possible."

Asenath drew in a breath, knowing what she had to say. "If I shouldn't have the seal, I can go get it right now and give it to you."

Dennis shook his head. "No, you have a right to it. You mentioned that you're learning to be a witch." Asenath nodded, and he went on: "When you're finished with your training, if you're interested, we can teach you some things. Of course you'll have to take the oath of the League and make some time for training, but the offer's open."

Asenath thanked him and then asked, "Will the seal open the way to Yian?"

"Not until you've learned how to use it," he said.

"Good." With a little shrug: "It's beautiful there but I'm not sure I want to go back, and I certainly don't want to end up there by accident."

* * *

Before dinner that evening, Robin said, "I read the cards this afternoon while you two were at Mrs. Sawyer's. Most of what I got I knew already—what kind of trouble I'm going to be in when I get back home, that sort of thing—but there was something kind of odd."

"Oh?" Mrs. Bishop looked up from the little cloth bag she was stuffing with herbs, a healing amulet for old Ruth Osborn.

"Yeah. Do any of the roads near here get much traffic any more?"

"The Aylesbury Pike gets some use again, now that the state highway's had two bridges fall down," said the witch. "A few dozen cars and trucks a day, or so I hear. Why?"

"The cards say that if I go to a road tomorow morning first thing, someone will come along who needs directions, and I'll get home sooner and they'll get where they need to go." He glanced up from his plate to Asenath. "But I can't go alone."

There had been discussions earlier that day about how to get Asenath, Robin, and Evan back to Arkham. The Quanyuan Hui would be leaving in another day, but they were going the opposite direction, east and north toward upstate New York. Evan's cousin-in-law Alan Sawyer had a pickup in working order, and could take all three of them and the two boys' bikes, but it would be three days before he could take time away from his job. Evan seemed happy with that, and Asenath knew why—she'd already heard amused gossip among the Dunwich folk about Evan and Cassie—but she wanted to get home as soon as she could. She'd thought about using the power Phauz had given her, but dismissed the idea regretfully; she couldn't risk anything that might reveal that secret.

Besides, there was Robin.

She turned to Mrs. Bishop. "Do you think it would be safe?"

"Unless Martha Price and Betty Hale are much poorer teachers than I have any reason to think," said the witch, "you ought to know more than enough to make it safe. Still, I can put a protection on the two of you if you'd like."

"Please," said Asenath. "I want to see how you cast one of those." Then, to Robin: "The card reading you gave me last week was really accurate, you know. First thing tomorrow?" He nodded, and she went on. "Let's do it."

The evening set an ordinary rhythm, punctuated by dinner in the kitchen, slices of pie in the parlor, a little quiet conversation, and then good-night wishes, trips to the little house out back and, for Asenath, the stair to a bedroom on the second floor. She said her prayers to Phauz, changed into a nightgown she'd borrowed from Mrs. Bishop—it hung on her like a tent, but it was good soft flannel and kept her warm—and settled under the covers of the narrow bed. It took her more time than usual to get to sleep, but that was because thoughts about Robin were circling in her mind. If she was wrong, and he wasn't actually in love with her—

She managed to get her mind stilled eventually, and sank into sleep.

Rachel was waiting for her in the *between* place, and the two of them made the leap to Ooth-Nargai without incident, blinking awake from something that was not sleep in a grove of ginkgo trees low on the slopes of Mount Aran. She'd planned on going on into Celephaïs that night and seeing if she could find a ship to take her across the Cerenerian Sea to visit good friends in the kingdom of Sydathria, but when she sat up she found that she and Rachel weren't alone in the ginkgo grove. A black dog sat there on its haunches, facing them in perfect silence. Long and lean, it had a pointed muzzle and pricked ears; its eyes were blank and featureless, like the eyes of a blind thing.

"Hi," Asenath said to it. "Do you know how to talk?"

The dog pointed with its muzzle to a trail that led up and around the slope of the mountain to the west, then got up, trotted to the mouth of the trail, and stood there waiting.

"Okay," Asenath replied, and got to her feet. Rachel, perched on her shoulder, let out a little uneasy chirr. "I know," Asenath told her. "But I think I know whose dog that is."

The dog, once it knew that she was following, trotted calmly ahead of her, leading the way up the trail. Overhead, morning sunlight streamed across the sky, lit the snows on the mountain's peak; golden birds darted from branch to branch and sang. Finally, as she half expected, she rounded a corner to find a broad place in the trail, a view to the west far out over the Cerenerian Sea, an ornate stone bench, and a tall figure dressed all in black who was seated on the bench, and gestured with a hand that glittered with rings, inviting her to sit beside him. The dog trotted off into the undergrowth and vanished.

"Lord Nyarlathotep," she said nervously, and curtseyed before sitting down.

"Thank you for accepting the task I set," the Crawling Chaos said. "It was time for the last holy thing from the Moon Temple of Irem to come back to the people of the Great Old Ones, and for two people to come back to the world as well. It's more usual for witches to begin taking on tasks for my masters when they have finished their training, but Phauz suggested otherwise in this case. It was a task well suited to your abilities: a little thing, in a sense."

Asenath nodded slowly. "I'm glad I could help." A pause, then: "Can I ask a question?"

The black unhuman eyes turned toward her. "Of course."

"The statue from Irem—my grandmother's statue." She paused a moment to try to gather her thoughts. "It's powerful, but it doesn't do anything the Radiance has to worry about.

I can feel that. Why did they do so much and kill so many people to try to get it?"

"You don't understand our enemies, I see."

"No," she admitted. "No, not at all."

"It's a simple matter." He turned, looked off across the Cerenerian Sea into distance. "They want humans to control the entire cosmos, to make it do what they want and only what they want. But the more control you have over a thing, the less of its own life it can have. Tell me this—would you want to control Robin Martense, to make him speak and do only when and what you willed?"

"Of course not," she said, shocked, and then suddenly blushed, realizing just how precisely the Crawling Chaos must know her unspoken thoughts.

"Exactly," said Nyarlathotep. "The members of the Radiance know that, too. They know that in order to control the cosmos, they would have to reduce it to a hollow shell of itself, stripped of everything that gives your species happiness. They tell themselves that it doesn't matter, that their grand dream is too important to be hindered by such trifles, but of course it does matter—and that's why they hunt down the sacred things of my masters with such frantic hatred. They want nothing to exist on this little Earth to remind anyone how full of life the world was before the Radiance arose, and how full of life it will be again once the Radiance is no more—nothing to remind them that all their efforts can accomplish is make the world a little emptier and a little more barren than it would have been."

Asenath took that in. "Okay," she said after a moment. "I understand—well, kind of." Wind stirred the ginkgos above them. "There'll be other tasks for me to do, won't there?"

"Of course. Phauz gave you the power she did for good reasons, and you've also been guided toward initiations and fields of lore that will be useful to my masters in times to come."

"The stone seal," she ventured.

"Among others. Will you take up Dennis Cooper's offer?"

"Yes, of course." Looking out to sea: "I love witchcraft, but I'd like to learn more than that. I love being an initiate, working with the Esoteric Order of Dagon and the Starry Wisdom Church, and I want to learn what the Quanyuan Hui teaches, too, but I want to do more than that, too. I don't even know if there's a word for what I want to be."

"Of course there is," Nyarlathotep said, imperturbable. "Sorceress."

She tried to speak, failed. After a moment: "Is—is that even something I can do?"

"The path was set before you before you learned to speak your first word."

Asenath stared at him for another moment, and began to understand. "Aunt Jenny."

"She saw the potential. Tsathoggua confirmed it. Phauz took over your guidance later." A gesture hinted at wheels within wheels, subtle plans ripening across the years, and in that moment Asenath knew part of what the architecture of events she'd sensed was meant to bring about; knew also that the events that shaped her life and destiny played only the smallest role in patterns far vaster, great wheeling movements that spanned ages and immensities.

"There are others," said Nyarlathotep then. "The time of the Radiance is drawing to its end at last, and when it's over, whatever happens, a great deal of hard work lies ahead. Sorcerers and sorceresses will be needed to do some of that work."

"Okay," said Asenath. "I want to help however I can." Then, gathering up all her courage: "Can I ask another question?"

The Great Old One considered her, nodded.

"Is it going to be any kind of problem if I get married?"

"That doesn't concern my masters at all," said Nyarlathotep. "Your grandmother desires offspring, of course, but she's utterly indifferent about how you get them."

"I know," said Asenath with a choked little laugh. "And she likes baby spiders and baby slugs as much as baby humans." She drew in a ragged breath. "Okay. What should I do now?"

"Return to your home and speak to no one about this. Jenny Chaudronnier will be told, and she'll approach you when the time is right. For now, you have plenty of work to do."

He stood up. "One other thing. Tomorrow morning you'll meet people you know. Answer their questions truthfully. It's time that they know more than they do."

Then all at once he was gone. Rachel let out a low chirr. "Yes, I know," said Asenath, and sat there for a long time before standing up and starting down the path toward the harbor of Celephaïs and the next stage of her dream-quest.

* * *

A dirt trail led through the woods from the covered bridge over the Miskatonic south of Dunwich to the Aylesbury Pike. Asenath had walked it many times and Robin twice, and so they had no trouble finding their way. Overhead the autumn sky unfolded in a glory of heraldic blue edged with clear morning sunlight. A hawk traced crisp mathematical curves through space, then soared off into distance. Once it was gone, sparrows darted through the undergrowth to either side of the trail.

All along the route, Asenath wondered which of them would find the courage to speak first. A few ordinary phrases of thanks and farewell had gotten them out of Dunwich, a few brief words had settled the necessary details of their route and timing, but silence followed as soon as those were said. Tension filled the air between them, crisp as ozone before a thunderstorm.

Half an hour after they left Dunwich, the trail ended at a parking lot decorated with the rusting remains of two long-dead cars. The gas station and mini-mart that once stood there had long since collapsed in on themselves, but the bench where the bus from Aylesbury used to stop was still intact on the far side of the road. Robin went over to it, motioned to her, sat down. "I don't think we have to wait long," he said. She perched on the bench, watched him, wondered what they were waiting for.

Minutes passed. He opened his mouth, closed it, looked away, and then finally said, "Yesterday, when Mrs. Bishop asked whether we'd done anything and—and you said that was for when we were married, that was a joke, right?"

"No," she said. "No, not at all."

"Come on." His voice went ragged. "You're the daughter of the Grand Priestess, and they're already saying you're going to be the best witch Arkham's had for a couple of hundred years. You could have anybody you want."

"I know," she said, and reached over to slip her hand around his.

His head jerked around. She met his gaze with a smile, and when disbelief showed too obviously in his eyes, nodded. He clenched his eyes shut, and after a moment, eyes still shut, his hand closed around hers.

More minutes passed. Neither of them moved. Wind gusted down the road, stirred up dust and sent dry leaves dancing ahead of it. Then, through the wind's sounds, another noise made itself heard: the low distant grumble of a diesel engine.

"Here comes our ride," Robin said then. Their hands parted, a little self-consciously. They stood up. Sunlight glinted off something off to the west, along the Aylesbury Pike. A minute or so passed, and it glinted again, closer. Another minute, and Asenath could see the oncoming windshield clearly enough to guess what was behind it.

She started to laugh. "You're really good."

"I drew the Rider, the Crossroads, and the House," said Robin, blushing. "That didn't take a lot of work to figure out."

The bus slowed as it came closer, groaned and rattled to a halt when it got level with them. As Asenath had guessed, the bus was bright purple beneath a layer of dust, with the word ORICHALC in white on the side. The door clanked and wheezed open, and Molly Wolejko came pelting down the stair. "Sennie, right?" she asked. "What the hell are you doing here?"

"Hi, Ms. Wolejko," Asenath said. "We were hoping to catch a ride to Arkham."

"Sweet. Guess where we're headed."

They climbed aboard the bus, and Asenath introduced Robin to the other members of the band. "Yeah, we got stuck in Montréal for a while," Molly said. "The engine went splat and Vern had to do a whole mess of work on it. It's been touch and go ever since." Her gesture dismissed the matter. "We'll stop where it gives out once and for all, and figure out what to do from there. In the meantime, yeah, Arkham's our next destination."

Once they were settled, Vern tried to start the engine again, got an unsteady whine and an ominous grinding noise, and had to get off the bus and spend a few minutes doing something with tools before a second try coaxed the engine to life. Thereafter the bus lurched into motion and started lumbering east over cracked pavement. Asenath and Robin sat on the long bench seat in the lounge, side by side. Molly flopped into a chair facing them and said, "So what the hell were you two doing out here in the middle of nowhere?"

"We were visiting friends in Dunwich," said Asenath. "It's a few miles up the road."

"Dunwich?" Howie said, from the table by the kitchenette. "There you go again, talking like we're in a story by H.P. Lovecraft."

"Maybe you are," Asenath said. Howie made a rude noise in his throat and turned back to the paperback he was reading.

Molly asked them about the route. After they'd explained that all the bus had to do was follow the Aylesbury Pike to its end, she went forward into the cab to let Vern know, and Asenath glanced at Robin to find him looking at her. He blushed and looked away, and she took his hand again, felt it tense and then relax around hers.

Sitting there, with Robin beside her and home only a few hours ahead, she let herself think about the long strange story that had ended at the Dunwich Starry Wisdom church. A little thing, Nyarlathotep had said, and of course he was right. The statue from Irem had been one of the least of the Moon Temple's treasures, of that Asenath had no doubt. Its powers, potent though they were, offered no answers for a troubled age; they wouldn't release Great Cthulhu from his tomb in drowned R'lyeh or even keep Dunwich safe from the Radiance. Yet the statue had mattered to Giles Rowley and to the other people who'd left Iceland and gone to their deaths to keep it safe; it had mattered to Clifford and Cassilda Whateley, to the elders and people in Dunwich, to her—and to Nyarlathotep the Crawling Chaos.

Robin's hand stirred in hers, and she glanced at him. That they'd sorted out what was between them, not turning back to the friendship they'd had as children but moving forward, toward something she could only guess at, something dim, uncertain, newborn—that was a little thing, too. Across the immensities of space and time that Asenath had studied in tomes of eldritch lore, whether or not she married Robin mattered no more than the doings of two grains of dust. Yet the grains of dust also had an opinion on the subject. Of that, too, she had no doubt.

Molly came back from the cab, sprawled in her chair again, and said, "Howie's right, you know. You and your dad both talk about stuff out of Lovecraft, Chambers, writers like that—but you don't talk about them like they're in stories. You talk about them like you've got shoggoths for neighbors and Deep Ones in the family tree." Robin choked, and Molly gave him a quick wry look and went on. "And I've seen enough here and there to really start to wonder. So—" She met Asenath's gaze. "Do you have shoggoths for neighbors?"

Asenath opened her mouth to answer and stopped, recalling Nyarlathotep's words. "Yes," she said. "Yes, we do."

Molly's purple eyebrows went up. Howie put his book down. "Seriously?"

"Yes," she said again, drew in a deep breath, and began to explain.

AUTHOR'S NOTE

This fantasia on a theme by H.P. Lovecraft belongs to the same fictive universe as my series of novels *The Weird of Hali* and shares many characters with those novels. Readers of that series may find it helpful, or at least interesting, to know that it begins a little less than eighteen years after the first volume, *The Weird of Hali: Innsmouth*, and a little more than two years before the start of the final volume, *The Weird of Hali: Arkham*. The "Narrative of Jan Maertens," which plays a role in this tale, was introduced in the third volume, *The Weird of Hali: Chorazin*, and other references to events in Greenland link back to themes introduced in *A Voyage to Hyperborea*. Since this is the last tale I intend to write in that tentacular cosmos, I have tried to draw together a few of the loose ends left dangling by my previous tales.

Like my other tales based on H.P. Lovecraft's Cthulhu mythos, this one depends even more than most fiction on the labors of other authors. Lovecraft himself contributed a great deal of the backstory, especially but not only by way of his stories "The Dunwich Horror" and "The Dream-Quest of Unknown Kadath," but an even larger share came from Robert W. Chambers, especially through his story "The Maker of Moons." That I took the other side in the quarrel Chambers sketched out will doubtless come as no surprise to my readers.

A few other debts deserve to be mentioned here. I am grateful to Carl Hood Jr. for his help with the badly garbled Chinese in Chambers' story, for the image of the seal that appears at the beginning of each chapter of this novel, for a great deal of information on Chinese alchemical and sorcerous traditions, and for a helpful reading and critique of the tale. A more personal debt is owed to Sara Greer, who also read and critiqued the manuscript. I hope it is unnecessary to remind the reader that none of the above are responsible in any way for the use I have made of their work.

Printed in the USA
CPSIA information can be obtained
at www.ICGtesting.com
JSHW032038260424
61991JS00007B/84

9 781915 952042